Unconditional

Encounters with Unexpected New Friends

by

Virginia A. Rockhill, Ph.D.

This is a work of fiction. All of the characters, organizations, and events portrayed in this novel are either products of the author's imagination or are used fictitiously.

UNCONDITIONAL

Encounters with Unexpected New Friends

Published by:

Three Sixteen Publishing
North Smithfield, RI 02896 USA

www.unconditionalstory.com

The Library of Congress Catalog Number:
2018908773

ISBN 978-0-692-16050-3
First Edition: September 2018
Printed in the United States of America

cover by Svetlana Osipova

for Abbie

Prologue

"We'll be done with this soon. Then all we have to do is let nature take its course. First the river animals will start to get sick, and as they do, they will have bred a few times. Their offspring will start to show genetic mutations. It's like we are creating our own species! You'll have your pick of animal skins you can sell. There are beaver, muskrat, raccoon, fox, rabbit, coyote and mink. Some snakes to skin too. You can make all sorts of things from reptile skins. Since that's always been a hobby of yours, you can pick whatever you'd like. The mutated animals won't be anything like their natural forms. They'll be much bigger and stronger, probably meaner too, just like the coyotes are. That's just to keep us busy until things get really interesting. It'll probably take six months or so before enough people notice there's a problem with the water. They'll blame the power company first, that will give things more time to, let's say, develop. The insects in the water will be the first to show effects, and when they breed, they lay hundreds of eggs. Then the small animals that eat the insects will be next. Of course anything drinking the river water will be affected as well."

"Are you sure this will work? We've got a lot riding on this", Juice asked. "I told you, this is my area of expertise. I have years of experience with genetic experiments. It's what other people do to plants with GMO. Think of it like GMA." "What's that?" Juice inquired, as he spat out the wog of saliva-soaked tobacco from his mouth onto the ground. "I would say that's short for Genetically Modified Animals," Professor Grimes laughed as he fantasized about how he would start new varieties of animals. "I still don't get how this will work, and what did you say about the coyotes?" Juice asked. "You fool! How many times have I told you to use the gloves I gave you when you are handling the chemicals? You and your chewing tobacco! If this stuff gets into your body, who knows what it will do to you" Professor Grimes yelled.

"How did you know I was here?" she excitedly asked the toad. He replied, "It was very much trial and error, but I remembered you complaining how much you didn't like leaving so early every Monday morning for the long ride down south. I would hear you going out by the side door with your human, and then the car driving out of the garage, up the driveway, and away. Then I wouldn't hear or smell you again until Friday night. Well, I got curious about where you went every week. I heard your human talking about going to some island every week and taking you with her. Then, you never came back anymore. It took some serious thinking about where you could be and should I go there too. It was lonesome without you up there, and somehow, something inside me said I should follow you. Fortunately for toads, we have a very good sense of direction and smell. I remembered how your smells changed after you got back home so I figured if I started out going south until I matched up the earth smells that were the same as yours, eventually I'd find you. It took me over two years! I really wish you would keep your face away from me, sometimes I think you're going to crush me. I didn't come all this way to get squashed by a Shih Tzu's face."

Abbie pulled back, but it was so hard because she was so happy to see Mr. Toad again. They had been acquaintances for a few years and had enjoyed romping and hopping around near the big blue door together. They were an unlikely pair of God's creatures, but then that could be said about so many living things. When Winter would come, which it did early above the 45th parallel, he would dig down well below the frost line, which was over 5 feet deep, sleep through the coldest months, and not come back out until the end of April, when most of the snow was gone and a few hardy insects had started to re-appear. He'd have quite the appetite by then, and would spend most of his time building his little body back up with the healthy proteins and fats the bugs would provide.

How he knew when to wake up from that deep slumber he could never figure out, but there was something inside him, someplace within him, that let him know it was time. He would feel like he wanted to stay hibernating, because, after all, he was an amphibian, and his body would be the same temperature as his little sleep nest. But, he trusted whatever it was that told him it was time to awaken and smell the fresh air again. Somehow, it seemed to be part of the same rhythm that the rest of the earth and plants followed. It was something that he knew he could trust because it made him feel safe. He wondered if other toads felt the same way.

"So how do you like it here?" he asked. "It's very different", she said. "At first, I was nervous about all the new noises, people and other dogs. The work schedule changed for my mom. That's her over there at the end of my leash. She's the one who introduced us to one another, remember? I do like living here better though, there's more to do. My job changed as well as my mom's." He seemed surprised at this, as he never knew she worked at all. "What do you mean you have a job? Shih-Tzu's are not known to be working dogs, everybody knows that. I thought you just laid around indoors on soft, fluffy things."

She looked at him through her long eyelashes, below the bows on the top of her head and said "If there was one thing I learned about people in my old job as co-therapist with my mom, it was that some people can change. It's not that they looked different, they're all the same breed, not like dogs, but I noticed that some of them seemed to not like themselves or other people, and this made them unhappy. It's not until I moved here and had the chance to make friends with other dogs that I realized that different breeds of dogs can be friends, so why do some humans dislike other humans, when they're all the same breed?"

When toads think, their wrinkly foreheads become even more wrinkly, making Mr. Toad look much older than his years. "Hmm, toads don't have this problem either. What do you think makes some humans like that?" She gave a deep sigh, as only Shih Tzu's can do, and said, "Well, I can tell you that in my spare time, my mom said I have earned a degree as a CEA. That is short for

Continual Environmental Analyst, and that is my new job. It's what I do now." "So do you analyze what people do?" he asked, as his tongue jumped out of his mouth grabbing a tiny mosquito that flew by as part of his breakfast. "Listen, I don't have a lot of time to talk now. Mom knows I have finished my business and she wants to take me back inside. This is my address on the third floor. She scratched the number on the ground with her paw. Do you think you can get up there by yourself?"

Chapter 2
The Rainbow Bridge

He had learned that the black Jeep was her mom's, and watched her drive off to work. Being so good at camouflaging himself so that rodents, snakes and some birds wouldn't devour him, he cautiously observed the comings and goings of the many people who lived in the big red brick building where Abbie now lived. There were many ways he could enter without anyone seeing him. He had a choice of stairways or these two small rooms that somehow went up and down all by themselves, with doors that slid open to each floor after a bell sound went off. He couldn't understand why anyone would want to go into these small, vertically moving rooms when all you had to do was hop up the stairs. He certainly didn't see anything like these where she had lived before. He decided there was no way he was going into one of them and possibly get crushed by the humans and dogs who went into them.

He arrived at the third floor, which he assumed was the top floor, because he ran out of stairs. He caught her scent on the floor so it was easy to find where she lived. As a toad, he didn't need to look for the door number; besides, he didn't want to tell her he couldn't read numbers anyway. Maybe if he had grown up down here, there would have been schools for toads to learn these things, but for now, he was eager to meet with Abbie without any humans around. He hoped there were no cats in her home, as cats definitely don't like toads! He hopped past many doors down the long hall, staying close to the wall. The thought of being found by a human who was afraid of toads or by another animal could have meant certain death. He noticed that there were no insects around, which would mean he couldn't stay too long up here or he'd starve.

He found her door on the left side of the hall. Since toads can compress their bodies quite flat, he was able to squeeze under the door, being glad he had not eaten too much for breakfast. She was waiting for him just a few feet within, lying on a couch with a bored expression on her flat face. "What took you so long?" she asked. "I had to hop up six flights of stairs, because each floor is about twice the height of a normal floor. Why is everything so high around here?" he grudgingly asked. "This place used to be some kind of factory where they made stuff a long time ago, long before my breed was even in this country and still in China. That's why everything is so big here." Looking around the space she called her home, he didn't think he could ever be comfortable there. He hopped from one area to another, sniffing as he went along, looking for a dark, damp corner to hide in if it became necessary. "You can look around all you'd like, my mom is out for the day, it's just the two of us here" she said. "Where does she go?" he asked. Abbie replied " She tells me she has to go to work and she would like to take me with her if she could, but if she did, she wouldn't be able to get any work done. I don't understand why, because I miss her when she's not here, but I know she'll come home. I spend my day either napping or managing the property from the loft windows upstairs. That's where my job is."

None of this made any sense to him at all. He didn't really know what a mom was; he could scarcely remember opening his eyes one day when he was in some kind of thick jelly sack, and then pushing through the sack another day. He had been on his own since then to find his own food, shelter and protection. Some memories of almost being crushed, eaten, starved, drowned or frozen helped him to acquire strong survival skills. He thought she probably never had experienced those kinds of dangers in her life. And what did she mean her breed hasn't been here that long. And where is China anyway? He was proud to say all the toads he had ever known had lived where he came from for who knows how many generations and weather cycles. "You mind if I go up to see where you, ahh, work?" "Not at all," she mumbled, almost falling back asleep. "Make yourself at home".

He found another long flight of stairs that she had nodded toward against the wall. These looked nice and soft, not like the hard stairs in the stairwells. It took a lot more effort to hop up each step because the soft stuff absorbed some of his energy, but he was determined to get to the top and look out the big floor-length windows he could see from the bottom of the stairs. She jumped off the couch and ran over to the stairs where he was. "Here, jump up on my back and I'll give you a ride up there," she said. Since she was short as well, although not as short as he was, it was an easy hop up onto her back. She ran up the steps, surprisingly fast, and walked over to a spot in front of one of the windows. He jumped down and stood next to her in amazement. He had never seen anything like this before! They were so high, it was impossible to see if there were any other toads on the ground. "Wow! What is it you do up here?" he asked. "Well," she said condescendingly, "This is where I work as a Continual Environmental Analyst, or CEA for short". "You mean this CEA thing really is your job?" he asked. He wasn't exactly sure what a job was anyway, but it seemed they were part of a whole different world, a world which was confusing, but somehow exciting as well. "It started off as a hobby, to give me something to do when mom is at work," she said. "But now I take it quite seriously, which is why I wanted you to come up and see for yourself. Besides, it can get lonely when I'm here all by myself."

She started explaining all the things she had taken notice of, but his eyes instinctively caught sight of some tiny bugs living on the huge plants in the room. His attention was captured by them, which resulted in the bugs being captured by his long tongue. "Hey, you're not listening!" she noticed his focus had shifted to the leaves of the adjacent tree. "You didn't tell me there'd be some food here," he said licking his narrow lips.

"What kind of stuff do you watch from up here?" he inquired, wondering if there were any more of those tiny little bugs on the tree to munch on. "There are humans taking their dogs out for walks, of course, and then there are some humans who go for walks without dogs, and there are other humans who run like someone is chasing them. I've never seen anyone actually chase another human, so I can't figure out what they are running away from, it looks like wasted energy to me." The bright sun was shining through the windows, which went right down to the floor, so they could both enjoy the warmth on their bodies. He was thinking maybe he could get used to this kind of life, not having to worry about being eaten, and having a handy food supply and a friend to hang out with. Would he have to get some special letters after his name as well? Come to think of it, he didn't even have a name. Her mom always called him Mr. Toad, maybe that was it. Would her mom become his mom too? He shook his little head; all this was getting to be more than he could consider right now.

He lay on his back, relaxed, with his little legs crossed, resting on his arms. "Did you ever wonder how it is that we can talk to one another, you know, because you're a dog and I'm a toad? I've never talked any other dogs," he said. "Now that you mention it, I've never talked to any other toads," she giggled. "I can understand most of what my mom says to me because of how her voice sounds and how she looks at me with love in her eyes. I know a lot of what actual words mean. With other humans, though, it's not easy to understand what they say. I get nervous around humans I don't know well." "I always get nervous with anything that is bigger than me, which is most things," he said. He surprised himself at being so honest about his feelings with her, realizing that his life was changing as they spoke.

He thought about other times when he felt some power or force that gave him a new way of looking at things and motivated him to try to improve the way he lived. It was like that when he decided to find Abbie after she moved away. It was a big decision to leave where he was born, but since toads lead very lonely, isolated lives, he didn't have much to leave behind. During his long journey to find her, he remembered that trusting, warm feeling that helped to guide him to her. What could that possibly mean? He decided to mention this to her and see what her thoughts were.

After considering what he told her, she said "Since I am a CEA, I pay attention to what humans say and do, as well as dogs and cats, and, well, other things too. There is a whole world that is invisible to humans but one which we can see. Some humans believe in this invisible world, even though they can't actually see it themselves. What you are referring to are the effects of this other world. Some humans call it the spiritual world. Many times humans think that dogs bark at nothing because the humans can't see anything, but dogs bark at things in this world invisible to humans. He wondered how she knew all this stuff, but he recognized that he had similar experiences, and when he chose to act on those guiding forces, good experiences resulted. What he hadn't known was that this world he could sense was not visible to humans, since he could sense both worlds.

He looked around to see if there was anyone else in the space with them. He didn't see anyone or anything. "Does this spiritual world visit here often?" he asked. "Yes, most of the time they are peaceful spirits. My mom says special words at night to protect us, she calls those words her prayers. They help to keep the good parts of the spiritual world here. Sometimes the spirits are animal spirits. They are friendly and like to hang out here with us. One is a red dog and another is a cat; they told me they were my mom's before they passed through the Rainbow Bridge. But I have seen and heard other parts of the spiritual world that frighten me. That's why I wanted you to come up here so we could talk. I always felt like we had some kind of bond between us, but I didn't know why or what it was."

Mr. Toad thought for a moment, wrinkling his rough brow again, and said, "What is a Rainbow Bridge?" Abbie answered, "It's something that happens to animals who have been loved very much by a human. This bond of love never dies because the bond somehow is attached to the human's spirit, which never dies and lives forever. So after the dog or animal's body dies, their spirit passes through the Rainbow Bridge. They can come back and visit their human whenever they want to. I know that someday I will pass through the Rainbow Bridge myself because my mom and dad take such good care of me and love me very much." This sounded fantastic to Mr. Toad, and he began to wonder if he would ever be loved enough to be able to get to this Rainbow Bridge place himself someday.

It was then that they both heard the door open and her mom walked in. "Oh no! I thought you said she'd be gone for the day and no one else would be here!" he said in a shaky voice. "She usually is gone all day, I don't know why she is home so early," Abbie whispered. "She's not afraid of toads, so I know she'd never do anything to hurt you, don't worry. Let's just stay right where we are, act like nothing is unusual and she'll come up and look for me like she always does. I'll just act the way I always do when she comes home and wag my tail."

Just as Abbie had said, her mom came up the soft covered stairs looking to find her. Mr. Toad moved a little closer to Abbie so he wouldn't get stepped on. Sure enough, her mom went right over to Abbie and started giving her kisses on her head and neck. He was shocked. He had heard stories about what happened to toads if they were kissed, and he wanted to stay just the way he was. Her mom noticed Mr. Toad and started saying how cute he was and how did he get all the way up here. She said something that maybe he hitched a ride on the stroller, whatever that was. Anyway, she saw that Abbie seemed happy that he was there and said not to worry, he could stay here after she bought some kind of thing for him to live in and food for him. After a few minutes, she went out again to buy his food and something called an aquarium which would be his new home.

"Phew," he said, "she really didn't mind that I was here." Abbie answered, "I told you she wouldn't. And you'll have your own place to live in here, where it will be safe for you. No more worrying about being eaten by snakes, birds or rodents. There is the vacuum cleaner though. I don't like that at all." "What's a vacuum cleaner?" he gulped as he asked the question. "It's this thing they use to clean the floor and stuff, that sucks up the dirt in this tube and makes a lot of noise." "Sounds more dangerous than being eaten" he said. "For you, only if you get in its way. You would have plenty of time to move into the house she's buying for you, it doesn't exactly sneak up on you. Remember, she doesn't know that we can speak to one another, she thinks I like you for the way you smell."

Some time later, her mom came back with a glass box that didn't have a top on it. She put some rocks, moss and plants in it with a tiny dish of water and then had some food that toads and frogs were supposed to like. Mr. Toad wasn't worried though since he knew that there were some delicious little bugs living on that tree near the big windows.

Chapter 3
The Sparkling Man

His first night was difficult, because being a toad, he was basically nocturnal. He could easily hop out of his new aquarium home, using the rocks that were strategically placed like toad-sized stairs up to its top. All the lights were off and Abbie was in bed sleeping, snoring loudly in fact. He used the darkness to explore the whole apartment. He could see that he was the only nocturnal creature there. He couldn't smell any rodents or crawling type bugs. It was warm enough in there and seemed safe to live in for all of them. He heard some occasional, far away barking from other dogs, but other than that, his new home was quiet. He felt like he belonged here, to Abbie and her mom, especially that he had his own space to retreat to when he needed to rest, drink and bathe. And there were those delicious tiny bugs on that tree, just waiting to be grabbed by his sticky tongue. Abbie was not interested in his aquarium, and said she didn't like the way it smelled after she stuck her nose in it once. He thought it was perfect and knew it belonged just to him.

He soon adjusted to the daily routines. It seemed that her mom went to work five days a week and was home on weekends. Mr. Toad and Abbie settled in to a daily schedule, in which he discovered she napped more than worked as a CEA. She started to teach him what letters and numbers are and how they get put together to spell words and other things. Abbie would go out to "do her business" four or five times a day and always came back happy and excited. He could never figure out why dogs got so excited when then came back from outside until he realized that Abbie's mom would give her a snack after she came in. Hmm, she never gave him a snack, but then he never went outside either. Then, there was always all that kissing on her head and telling her how cute and good she is. He was unsure if he would like to have all the attention that was lavished upon Abbie for himself. He discovered she had another dog friend who was also a Shih Tzu, whose name was Maggie and lived down the hall. They would play and chase each other around when together.

A couple of times Maggie would venture over to the aquarium to watch Mr. Toad if he was resting, but Abbie would lead her away from it because she knew Mr. Toad was still afraid of other dogs.

The seasons changed and winter arrived. This was the first winter he was not spending in hibernation. He did notice he spent more time sleeping, but with a constant warm environment, there was no need to hibernate. Every once in awhile, he would smell a cat who lived a few apartments down the hall walk by his door. The cat never seemed interested in entering his adopted family's apartment, but it still made him uneasy. There was another dog who lived right next door, who was a lot bigger than Abbie and seven other dogs on their end of the hall, including Maggie. They all seemed to get along with one another, playing and chasing one another when they had the chance.

One day when they were sitting in front of their favorite window, Mr. Toad thought he felt something moving by them which was part of the invisible world that humans can't see. He noticed a pleasant sensation, not at all uncomfortable. "Did you feel that?" he asked Abbie, who was taking a nap-break from her CEA job. "I didn't see anything, but I felt a safe, warm feeling go by," she said. He was becoming more and more curious about this other world which was more prevalent here in the big red brick building than it had been in the North Woods. Whatever or whoever they were, they seemed to enjoy being in the space with Abbie and him. He wondered if the invisible world visited all the other dogs on the floor as well.

One night, during one of Mr. Toad's nocturnal excursions, he hopped past his favorite spot on the soft fluffy part of the floor, which he had by now learned was called carpeting. This was right next to a different part of the brick wall, which had a section that didn't exactly match the rest of the bricks. He decided to get a closer look at this section, as there was nothing else to do. He leapt over and noticed that there was a small part of the mortar that was more powdery and had started to crumble in the corner. He thought this might have been a nice hiding place for bugs so he started to dig out the mortar. He dug enthusiastically for a few minutes when suddenly, a big clump gave way and he found that the energy he had put into digging was enough to propel his little body into a dark space. He noticed that it was a narrow stairway leading up toward the roof. He had no difficulty seeing in the darkness and had become very adept at leaping up stairs by now, so he decided to investigate.

The room looked and smelled like it had been used by humans recently. There were some books and papers on surfaces the same height as kitchen counters. There were glass bottles, containers, and papers with different kinds of numbers written all over them. It was not a tidy place, and looked like whoever had been using it must have been in a hurry to leave. He thought he'd just hop over to the other side of the room when he noticed that he was feeling that warm, pleasant feeling again. He decided to get closer because it seemed more comfortable on that side of the room. He couldn't smell anything harmful or edible, but he noticed that a light began to slowly shine where that the peaceful feeling was. It shone brighter and brighter until it was so bright, he couldn't stare at it any more. Covering his eyes with his tiny hands, he realized it was someone who sort of looked like a human, but different. It looked like a man who was made of some powerful light rather than a human body.

Mr. Toad was starting think maybe this midnight excursion wasn't such a good idea, when the Sparkling Man spoke to him. His voice was different than a regular human's, and had a powerful, but soft, sound to it. "Welcome, my little friend," it said. Mr. Toad said "Th-Th-Thank you," because he was feeling quite overwhelmed by now. The brightness in the room was unlike anything he had ever experienced before. "You are Mr. Toad, am I right?" the tall, lovely Light Person said. "I'm sorry if I disturbed you, I was just going for a midnight wander, hoping to find a different variety of bugs." "You needn't be afraid of me, I have spoken to many other humans and creatures in the past. My name is Gabe."

Mr. Toad had never met anyone like the Light Man before. His curiosity led him to ask "Do you live here?" Gabe said, "No, but I visit here as well as other places. That's part of my job. I live mostly in the world invisible to humans, but there have been times when I have visited the visible world of humans as well." Mr. Toad's attention was probably never as focused as it was while Gabe spoke to him. He continued, "The world today can be so confusing to humans that many of them have lost their way and can't recognize the Truth. They place so many of their beliefs in temporary experiences that they think will bring them happiness, only to become lonely, disappointed or angry. Of course, it is their very own choices to pursue those experiences. Unfortunately they are frequently misguided by harmful forces."

Mr. Toad asked "Pardon me, please, but I don't understand what you do when you visit the human world." "Usually it is to bring someone a very important message or idea, perhaps one that they have tried to ignore, but must hear and should act upon," he said. Mr. Toad's parotid glands on his back began to itch when he heard this, which they frequently did when he thought very hard. He remembered that the warm safe feelings he now had were the same ones he had back in the North Country when he decided to find Abbie. "So YOU brought me a message to come here?" he asked. Gabe didn't have to use words to let Mr. Toad know the answer to his question. He said, "You can think of me as a messenger from the Creator, the Father of all life."

Mr. Toad asked, "Do you visit this place often?" Gabe said "I have permission that I can visit here as often as is necessary. It doesn't take me long to get here, so if you would like, I can come back another time." Since meeting Gabe, Mr. Toad had never felt such tranquility. "Yes, I would like to meet with you again. Can you come up here another time?" he asked. Gabe answered. "I can meet you anywhere, but I don't think your friend Abbie could fit through that crack in the mortar like you did. How about I meet you where you live?"

Mr. Toad found himself staring straight ahead for a few minutes and thought that he must have fallen asleep and dreamt about Gabe, the Sparkling Man. He was still feeling peaceful and excited, at the same time. He realized that he had never felt that way before, so he must have been actually speaking with him. The space he was in had become dark again after Gabe had left. He really didn't remember exactly how he left, but he was alone now. He jumped up and found the stairway, hopping back down and through the little space that opened between the brick wall and floor. It seemed like he had been gone for hours and that it should have been daylight by now, but everything was still in darkness as he heard Abbie gently snoring in bed.

Chapter 4
The Folded Crystal

The next morning, after Abbie's mom went to work, he hopped out of his aquarium home to join Abbie next to their favorite window. She was already working at her CEA job. "You'll never guess what I discovered last night!" he said to her. "I was just hopping around, you know, looking for some midnight snacks on these big plants. I don't know what made me look at a place on the brick wall or what made me start to dig around there, but anyway, I ended up on the other side of the brick wall, where there is a stairway, and I met someone who was all bright and shiny and he said his name was Gabe and he wants to speak with us. He said he'd come to see us here if we would want that." Abbie was perplexed. She had never heard Mr. Toad talk so excitedly and fast before. "Are you sure you were not dreaming?" she asked. "I wondered that myself, but I noticed that when I was with him, I felt very happy and calm, like the way I think a perfect world would make you feel like. It was sort of like the way we feel when the peaceful spirits from the invisible world are here, but much stronger," he said.

Abbie still wondered if Mr. Toad really did have a dream. Could this have happened? Is there really something behind this wall that she had been sitting next to for the past two years and not noticed? She walked over, pushing her tiny nostrils into the space that her amphibian friend had pointed to. The powdered mortar made her sneeze, and all she could smell was where Mr. Toad had crawled through the crack. She was curious, however, and thought it wouldn't hurt if they invited Gabe to visit with them. As long as he came when they were alone. But how could he get into the apartment? Neither she nor Mr. Toad could open the door by themselves; it was usually locked anyway. "Did he say how we could get back in touch with him?" she asked Mr. Toad. "Umm, I forgot to ask that," he said.

The next evening Mr. Toad went for his usual midnight walk around the apartment. He pushed through the crumbled mortar again and hopped up the stairs to the empty room. He was hoping to find Gabe there again but he was disappointed when he did not find him. He thought he would look around the dusty room, but all he saw were the soiled books and papers on the counter tops. It was very quiet and still, and he noticed he didn't feel as safe as when Gabe was there. He became discouraged and decided to go back down to the apartment and go to sleep.

Later that morning, he asked Abbie "Do you think I'll ever see Gabe again?" "Did he say he would definitely contact you?" she asked. "Not exactly," he said. He was starting to feel foolish, like maybe it really was just an unusually vivid dream. After all, who had ever heard of someone with so much bright light coming out of his body. "I wish he would come here. I have so many questions to ask him; he seemed to be very smart about a lot of stuff." Abbie asked "Like what?" "Well, I always wondered why I had a strong feeling to find you after you left, and how it was that I eventually did find you. He said he helped me with that." Abbie suddenly jumped up and turned her head like she heard something in the apartment. "Shhh!" she softly growled. Mr. Toad hopped toward the direction she was now facing. Then they both saw it happen together. A few feet in front of them, it looked like a very bright light was unfolding from some crystal shape. Within a few seconds, the brightness became the Sparkling Man. "GABE!" Mr. Toad shouted. "It's you!"

Gabe smiled at both of them saying "I have been right here all along, but, you couldn't see me." Abbie kept staring at him with her little mouth open, thinking he was the most beautiful thing she had ever seen. She usually was very shy with someone she didn't know, but he seemed so perfect and safe, all she wanted was to stay close to the bright light that surrounded him. Her little nostrils were working hard to identify the strange, pleasant fragrance that encompassed him; her skin felt the warmth from his light, and she noticed that his voice was unlike any other sound she had ever heard. She knew that now that she had met him, her life would never be the same and she never wanted him to leave her.

"Hhhhow did you do that? Wh-where did you come from? I'm sorry, I don't mean to be rude, but am

I dreaming or hallucinating?" Mr. Toad asked the Sparkling Man. Gabe smiled gently and said "You wanted me to visit with you both and I have been waiting for you to ask." This was one of those rare times Abbie was speechless. Gabe seemed to know what both of them were thinking. He looked right at Abbie and said "Most dogs can usually sense when someone from the world invisible to humans passes very closely." She wasn't sure if she spoke or just thought her response, "But I've never seen anyone like you before." He reached over to gently rub her head, saying "You are right. We have never met face to face before, but you have sensed others from my world."

Mr. Toad's parotid glands were about to melt off his back from thinking so hard. "So where do you live?" he asked. Abbie interrupted him saying "Wait, don't you see? The world invisible to humans is part of that bright crystal thing." Gabe said "It's not necessary that you understand where I came from, but you are right, Abbie. You can sort of imagine that this other world is folded up in that crystal shape that seemed like it was right in front of you. In fact, your world is just a part of that crystal too. You just can't notice because it is so tightly folded up within that crystal shape.

"Do you come here often?" Abbie asked. "More often than you would think," Gabe answered. "Remember when I said I am a messenger from the Creator of this world? Well, I have been making visits here for thousands of years, that's human years, not dog or toad years. You see, everyone on earth has a purpose and is part of the Creator's Plan, but many times some creatures don't know what their purpose is or what life on earth is really all about. It may seem easy for you both, but for a lot of humans, there are too many distractions and deceptions which confuse them, and they end up making choices that are hurtful to themselves and others. The more confused they get, the more they are unable to find their own purpose."

"Do we have a purpose?" Mr. Toad asked Abbie. She said, "Of course we do. We're supposed to love our humans, no matter what, everybody knows that's what dogs do best." "But I'm not a dog," he flatly replied. "That's true," Gabe said, "but did you ever think you are a good friend to Abbie? Isn't that having a purpose in life? And by being her friend, you now have a safe place to live. See how it can work when you accept one another for who you are? In the beginning, that was the way things on earth were supposed to be for all creatures, so that everyone could live together in trust and harmony. But the first humans unfortunately made a choice which hurt themselves and eventually everything else on earth." "Wow! what kind of choice did they make?"asked Mr. Toad. Gabe went on to explain that the first humans decided to ignore the one rule that was given to them by their Creator, and by doing this, permanently separated themselves, and everyone after them, from a perfect existence on earth.

Abbie and Mr. Toad sat there deeply in thought. They had no idea that this choice some people made a long time ago resulted in so many problems for the world today. They had both heard people talking about confusing things happening in the world, but didn't know that it all began thousands of years ago. "What about kids, do they get confused and deceived too?" Abbie asked, thinking about Bella and Lizzy, who she likes to play with when they visit her mom. Gabe said "There are always circumstances that can bring confusion and deceit into everyone's lives, making it hard to recognize the Truth. My role as a messenger is to help communicate the will of the Creator." "So are we part of you doing your messenger job?" Mr. Toad asked. "If you both believe in my message and seek the Truth, you will have helped restore the natural order to the environment where you live." With that, Gabe smiled at them, and slowly disappeared back into the crystal.

Chapter 5

Choices

The idea that they were being given a choice rather surprised Abbie and Mr. Toad. Neither of them had ever before considered they had many choices in their lives, but since they had met Gabe, they began talking more about what their purpose was in life. He told them they would probably have some doubts about believing what he said, which would make them question how they could ever help others because they were only two small creatures. This is how the cycle of being separated from the Creator worked, making self-centered choices that would result in temporary outcomes instead of recognizing the will of the Creator, which would result in true, permanent happiness.

They wondered if they would see Gabe again, and thought about what he had said about becoming confused. In fact, they had even discussed if they had only day-dreamed or imagined him. They were both more sentient of the invisible world since Gabe had visited, and because of this, they decided he actually did visit and speak with them. They decided they would help him with this environment thing, whatever it was. They couldn't understand how two very small animals could somehow make a difference in the world, and why them, when there were so many other dogs and toads in the world. They didn't think there were any other toads in the big red brick building, but there were lots of other dogs and cats. Would they or other animals be part of this message as well?

The days seemed as though they dragged by, with Winter becoming Spring. Each morning they awoke, wondering if Gabe would speak with them again, only to be disappointed when nighttime came and he did not appear. Abbie and Mr. Toad had become inseparable. When she would go outside "to be a good girl" with her mom or dad, Mr. Toad thought about going out there with her, but he remembered her mom saying that he should not be allowed to leave the apartment because it might not be safe for him. He couldn't understand why; after all, he had always lived on his own before coming to live with Abbie. Part of him longed to hop around in the soft grass, sniffing out varieties of insects. He was getting bored with the food her mom provided him, always the same kinds of insects. He found himself staring out the big window, looking down at the wooded area that led down to the river. Ahhh, the river! He hadn't gone for a swim in a few years. All he had was the bowl of water in his glass box of a home. He thought about what it would be like for himself and Abbie to spend a day outside together. He knew she did go out, but it was always with her mom or dad. He was never included.

One morning, he decided he would hop onto the bottom of her stroller where he could not be easily seen when Abbie was going outside. As usual, Abbie was still sleeping in bed when it was time for her mom to take her out. No one expected to see him there as he usually didn't become very active until later in the morning. The little doggie stroller with Abbie in it and Mr. Toad hiding in the lower basket rumbled down the long corridor until they came to that moving room, which he now had learned was called an elevator. Before he knew it, they were outside on a bright Spring morning, with birds singing, which he knew meant available insects, as that is a big reason why birds sing in the morning. The stroller stopped, and Abbie was placed on the ground to sniff around and find whatever it was she was looking to find. He thought now was his moment, so he hopped out and away from the stroller to do some sniffing for himself.

The cool grass felt and smelled better than he had remembered it all those years of living outside. He felt like a real toad again, and when he spotted one of his favorite insects, he hopped over to catch it for the first course of breakfast. A few feet away, he noticed a hatch of other insects just crawling out of their eggs, and thought they would make a tasty main course. Before he realized it, he had hopped too far from the stroller to be able to jump back in. He looked around while swallowing his buggy feast, and could not see the stroller or Abbie! Oh, now what would he do? He decided all he had to do was wait around for Abbie to come back in the afternoon and then just jump back on the stroller and go back to the apartment with her. Until then, he would explore the area and hop down to the river and go for a swim.

Abbie and her mom returned to the apartment as they always did. She had her breakfast, and her mom left for work. Abbie walked up the stairs to the loft area to start her job as a CEA and wait for Mr. Toad to join her. Little did she know that as she looked out the big window overlooking the river below, Mr. Toad was eagerly hopping toward it, with no thoughts of the dangers he was about to encounter.

Midday came, and Abbie realized Mr. Toad had not hopped beside her on her window cushion. She decided to go downstairs and look for him. He wasn't in his aquarium or anywhere else. She became worried and frantically searched for him everyplace she could reach. She called his name, (which sounded like barking to humans, but not to the other dogs on the floor). After a few hours of scouring the apartment, she had to lie down. She whimpered loudly because she feared he had either died or was somehow caught by one of the cats in the building. She was surprised at how much their friendship meant to her and how much he had become a part of her life.

Chapter 6

The Muskrat

Looking up at the blue sky and eagerly anticipating a fresh catch of river insects as he leisurely walked across the road toward the sloping hillside, Mr. Toad turned toward a roaring sound which was bearing down on him. His froze in fear, staring at a large truck moving right at his little body. He had seen these things on the road from the big windows where he and Abbie would spend hours next to each other in the safety of the apartment. She had told him these things were called tractor trailer trucks and had eighteen wheels and would carry loads of stuff from one location to another. She didn't know why there were so many of them, or why there was so much stuff to be carried around, but she said they were probably something to stay away from or else risk getting squashed like a bug. At the time, Mr. Toad thought that would be such a waste of an insect, but right now all he could think of was not being crushed himself. Fortunately for him, being paralyzed by fear and unable to hop, saved his life. The huge truck rolled right above him, and all eighteen wheels just missed his compact torso. He felt the vibration and the swirling sand pepper the skin on his back. He had never heard anything so loud before.

As the truck drove out of sight, Mr. Toad realized he needed to get out of the road before another truck came by. He quickly hopped to the curb where the grass began, when he heard a voice say, "I thought you were going to be like that frog last year who tried to cross the road. Boy-oh-boy, what a mess, frog parts all over the place, just splattered all over, it almost ruined my appetite for days I tell you. You just would not believe how ugly and messy it was…" "OK, OK, I don't need to know any more, just stop there with the details if you don't mind," said Mr. Toad, still shaking from his near miss with death. He looked up to see where the voice was coming from, to find it was a large, dark brown, male muskrat, chewing on some grass, staring down at him. "You don't need to be afraid of me, sonny, I don't eat toads, frogs, salamanders or any of your relatives." "I think I've seen you before, from up there," said Mr. Toad, pointing to the windows of the red brick building. "Yeah, everyone knows me around here, I've lived here for a few years. It's a great place to call home, lots of food, lots of land for tunnels in the winter, a quick place to hide, and a short cut to the river." "A short cut to the river?" Mr. Toad wondered. By now he just wanted to get as far away from that road as he could. "Sure, that's where you are headed I presume?" the muskrat queried. "It is, would you mind showing me?" he asked. "Just follow me, it's dark of course, but stay behind me so I won't run you over as we go down the hill, it's a steep tunnel."

The furry muskrat walked to the edge of the grass where the shrubs and tree canopies met, and slowly dove in the hole in the ground. Mr. Toad followed, wondering what he was getting himself into. Here he was, following a muskrat that he just met into the earth, not really knowing what he would find at the other end, if there was another end. But it was too late to turn back now. This did seem more safe than crossing that road again. He had a brief thought if he would ever be able to return to the cozy apartment again, but he pushed the thought out of his head as he felt himself begin to roll down the tunnel, trying to stay away from the muskrat's rear legs so he wouldn't get skewered by the sharp claws.

Chapter 7
Strange Animals

The bright sunlight almost blinded him as he rolled among the soft, tall grass blades upside down, with a bounce. The muskrat began to shake the dirt off himself, and proceeded to introduce Mr. Toad to the other muskrats. They seemed unimpressed, watching him while they chewed on the vegetation around them. The muskrat explained how he had met the toad and how he wanted to get down to the river for lunch and a swim. They all nodded while munching, not stopping to speak, as if they were in a hurry to finish their mid-day meal. The muskrat explained that they have certain areas to graze at certain times of the day, when it was most safe for them to eat. "We've learned that there are some animals and humans who are intent on harming us, or worse, so we've figured out where we have the best chances of not being injured or killed. As you can see, muskrats are all very handsome, but we can't run as fast as other animals like foxes, coyotes, dogs and cats. Then there are the humans who want to kill us for our warm furry coats. That's why we have our tunnels, not only for shortcuts, but for protection as well."

Mr. Toad had all but forgotten about the natural predators for toads while he was living with Abbie in the safety of the apartment. He really never gave much thought that other animals had to worry about being prey as well. He was so deep in thought about this that he didn't notice a rabbit had hopped right next to him. "I saw you almost become a toad-burger up there on the road, didn't you hear that thing coming toward you?" the rabbit asked. "I-I-I-I guess I just wasn't paying attention," Mr. Toad said, embarrassed. He found himself thinking about Gabe's words to him, about being separated from the Great Creator, the resulting deception, confusion, and about bringing a message to him and Abbie. He remembered the warm, safe feeling he had when Gabe was there, and how he didn't feel that way now. He wondered if the invisible world Gabe spoke about was down here at the river's edge too. It seemed like such a long time had passed since he was out of the apartment with Abbie. He looked up and noticed that the muskrats and the rabbit had all stopped eating and were staring at him. "Are you all right? You look like you're awake, but you're not acting like you are," the tawny-colored rabbit gently said. Mr. Toad decided he would tell them about Gabe and how he appeared to them. He needed to know if the invisible world visited the river.

"So you felt like you never felt before when you were with this Gabe person, like he was no danger to you and this made you feel safe and warm inside? And he would just appear, no noise, sound or smell, just very bright and he sparkled?" the muskrat asked. He didn't really know what the word "sparkling" meant, but he was trying to use his imagination. "You know when the moon is really bright, there are no clouds and it shines on the currents of the water? That's sort of what sparkling looks like, but much brighter than that," Mr. Toad described. He went on to tell them about his good friend, Abbie, and how they had met a few years before and how something inside him encouraged him to go find her at her new home.

"Have any of you ever felt like there was a good feeling inside of you that gave you an idea that you should follow, no matter where it led you?" he asked. "I sometimes wish I could do something about the changes we see here in our neighborhood, but I never thought there was something that I could really do about it," the large female muskrat said. He later learned that her name was Violet, the little rabbit was Opal and the large male muskrat's name was Slade. "What kind of changes do you mean?" Mr. Toad asked Violet. "Well, I've seen some new faces around here that just don't look exactly right. You noticed them too, didn't you Slade?" Violet asked. "Yup, I sure did. Sort of looked a little like a sick raccoon, huge, he was, couldn't move very fast, which was good because he looked at me like he wanted take a bite of out me. Never had that feeling before with a raccoon, it was kinda creepy, you know what I mean?" Slade said.

Their attention was interrupted by the flapping wings of baby geese, who were having trouble paddling onto the shore. Their bills were too big for their bodies, so their heads kept falling into the water, and their feet were not big enough to swim through the river currents. The swift water took some of them downstream, not being able to walk to land. Three of them made it onto the river's edge, a few yards away from Mr. Toad and his new friends. The goslings were panting with exhaustion, and Violet noticed they were very thin, like they hadn't been able to eat. They lay on their sides, looking like goslings, but then not looking like baby geese at all. Violet became very sad, wondering if she would have baby muskrats that didn't look like her or Slade. She was trying to understand how this could happen, because there were more and more occasions of things that were somehow changing.

Just then a group of very large dragonflies swooped over Mr. Toad. He realized he was hungry and just as his long tongue was about to grab one of the big dragonflies, Opal hopped over and rolled him over so he missed capturing the insect. "What are you doing, why did you do that?" Mr. Toad testily asked the rabbit. "I don't know why, something just told me to stop you from eating that big bug. What's the big deal, there is no shortage of insects for you to eat", she said. Mr. Toad remembered when he himself had experienced a thought to do or not to do something, and wondered if Opal had the same kind of awareness. It made him feel uneasy, missing Gabe even more. "Let's move away from here and get into one of the tunnels, where it's safe," Slade said to the little group. They had all started to feel like there was something too unnatural about the changes.

They walked, hopped and hobbled into another tunnel entrance, following Slade up the hillside after he covered up the opening with loam and rocks. It was completely dark but seemed safe from whatever it was outside that made them all shiver with fear. Slade knew all the twists and turns by heart, since it was he who had dug the tunnels over the past years. Since Mr. Toad was the littlest one of the group, he had to work the hardest to keep up. Finally the tunnel flattened out into a large area which had some faint light coming through the roof. "This is under the root structure of one of the biggest oak trees around here. Plenty of fresh air, a little stream in the corner for a drink or shower and lots of food stored for when the weather gets too cold to go out," Slade proudly announced. Mr. Toad thought this was indeed a great place to call home with all these amenities. He thought back to his apartment with Abbie and wondered if she was working at her CEA job. It occurred to him that she might have seen some of what was happening at the river's edge from the big window. As the little group was about to fall asleep, they heard the screams of terrified animals, which seemed louder and closer tonight. Somehow, he had to get back to her and let her know what they had seen.

Chapter 8
The Creator's Plan

Abbie had trouble falling asleep that night. Not only was she worried about where Mr. Toad was and if he was still alive, but she sensed an uneasiness in the building, especially in the area where Mr. Toad had said he found the stairway up to the room near the roof. She kept staring toward it, and was sure she sensed something from the visible world up there that made her anxious. Her ears were standing out straight, straining to hear what sounded like two men arguing with one another. There were lots of other people who lived in the big red brick building, but she had never heard anyone so angry before. She jumped out of bed and ran down the stairs to get away. Her mom had awakened because Abbie was restless, but Abbie knew her mom could not hear what she was hearing.

She ran into the little room where the washer and dryer were because there was a nice dark corner for her to hide in. She began to shake, whimper and feel very cold, wishing there was some way she could calm down. Suddenly, she thought about Gabe, and without realizing it, she said his name out loud. Within a second or two, she felt that peaceful, safe feeling sweep over her, and saw his unmistakable face moving out of the bright unfolding crystal, followed by the rest of his body. "I was waiting for you or your toad friend to call me," he said. She jumped onto his lap, feeling that everything was now perfect. She said, "Everything's been terrible today, I don't know where Mr. Toad went or if he is still alive. Even my mom has been looking for him. She even looked inside the vacuum cleaner bag and he wasn't there. And tonight, I heard some men yelling at one another up in the room that Mr. Toad found. I'm so glad you are here!"

Gabe stared into her eyes and she felt his pure love for her. "First, I can tell you that your little toad friend is alive and safe. At the moment, he is in an underground tunnel with two muskrats and a little rabbit. Actually, you know the big oak tree straight outside your big window upstairs? He is under that tree for the night." "How did he get there?" she asked. Gabe replied, "He got there by being too curious, and not paying attention, which is how most people get into trouble. Anyway, he needs to get back here with you."

Gabe went on, "Remember when I told you both that if you chose to help restore the natural order to the environment where you live, you would be choosing to live according to the Creator's plan? The Natural world was made to be perfectly balanced and peaceful. But, now there are forces which literally want to destroy the environment for all living creatures, animals and plants." "Are you saying that is what I was sensing tonight?" Abbie asked. "Yes, it was. This area was chosen by someone because the damage that has already begun won't be completely noticed until it spreads to other areas, affecting the water and food supplies," Gabe said. Abbie noticed that as Gabe spoke these words, there was not only seriousness in his voice and sadness in his eyes, but a sense of determination and power. "That abandoned laboratory up in the tower that Mr. Toad found is where the damage to the environment was conceived. I don't need to tell you how this all started right now, but I will tell you that when people falsely believe that they can control the world by changing its natural order, the result is chaos, death and destruction, which is the opposite of Creation.

For the first time, Abbie realized that Gabe really was the messenger of the One who had created the world. She couldn't imagine what this Creator was like. She had never thought about who created the first dogs, cats, toads, horses, cows, deer, moose and birds. These were the only other animals she had ever met, but she had seen images of other animals on television in the apartment, and knew there were many other different creatures.

"How is this destruction going to happen? Will it happen to everyone? Can it be stopped?" Abbie asked. Gabe took a deep breath, exhaling tiny speckles of pure light, which tumbled down over her face. She felt his tenderness and power mixed together, and knew that she wanted to be part of his message about Truth. Gabe answered "The person who is responsible for this plan wants to change the way plants and animals are actually formed and appear. Anything that ingests the water that has been polluted by him would undergo these changes. The worst part is that once these changes have occurred, they will be passed on to future generations of plants, animals, fish, insects and so on, so that in time, all naturally created life will become altered into unnatural lifeforms. It will take time for this to occur, but the longer he is allowed to continue his plan, there will be more destruction to the creatures of the earth. We have already seen some poor animals affected by this evil. They aren't aware why they are different, but they know they are having trouble surviving in their own environment," Gabe explained.

"Why would anyone want to change the way the earth is?" Abbie wondered aloud. Gabe answered, "There is only one Creator. Some humans believe that they can be creators, but in reality, this is a deception, a lie. Trying to rearrange life is not creating life, and in fact only leads to the destruction of life. There are many instances of Divine Inspiration, when someone is given some wisdom or talent by the Creator, to help improve life on earth." "What do you mean?" Abbie asked, her little eyebrows wrinkled together in thought. "Well, all through history, there have been some people who have had very important ideas that they couldn't have had on their own, they sort of needed some help to think in ways that were not humanly possible. The major breakthroughs in science, mathematics and music are just a few examples," Gabe said. "There are also regular people who have had ideas that seemed to just pop into their heads, that they should do something to lead others out of danger, or invent something that saves the lives of thousands." "What does all that have to do with the Truth?" she asked. Gabe answered "The Truth is anything that comes from the Creator to help people follow His Natural Laws, so that creatures of the earth can live together in love, peace and harmony. This is really much easier for animals than humans, who are always trying to change the earth to suit their own needs. The preferences of animals to live according to the way they were designed to live helps them to share the earth better than humans do." "Is that why Mr. Toad and I can help with your message?" Abbie asked. "Exactly," Gabe said. "But first we need to get that toad back here with you."

Chapter 9

Homesick

Mr. Toad had found a comfortably soft, damp spot in Slade and Violet's burrow. After a satisfying meal of a variety of bugs crawling within striking distance of his long tongue, he settled in for a good night's sleep. Opal was curled up a few feet away, and the two muskrats were snoring loudly next to one another on a soft bed of moss and mulch. He was grateful for their friendship and helpfulness in leading him to safety and sharing their little home with him. He wondered what it was that made them want to help him, just an ordinary toad. After all, they didn't have to invite him into their burrow, risking some danger to themselves in helping to protect him.

He thought about Abbie and if she was sleeping in bed, snoring as she usually did in a deep slumber. Did she notice he wasn't there? Did she miss him?

Did her mom notice he wasn't there? And what was it that made him leave the safety and comfort of the apartment? Oh yes, now he remembered, just to get outside for a greater variety of insects. He noticed he was having new feelings: loneliness, a sadness, an emptiness which seemed like they soaked through every part of his body. Here he was with three new friends, but he found he missed Abbie so much that his very being ached. He decided he would have to return to the apartment in the morning.

Chapter 10
The Storm Drain

Mr. Toad awoke to Violet's voice while she gathered some vegetation within the burrow for breakfast. She was speaking with Slade about how they should plan their day. He had already wandered down the tunnel to the river, having returned very distraught at what he had seen. "There were six or eight animals who had been skinned, their lifeless bodies left on the ground. I'm not sure if we even knew them, not being able to recognize them the way they are now. I know at least two of them were rabbits. I thought I heard some crying and screaming from the river last night," he said sadly. Violet seemed very worried, adding "I don't think it's safe for us to leave the way we came into the burrow. Who knows what or who is still out there." Mr. Toad jumped up hearing about the animals being skinned. "Is there another way out?" Mr. Toad asked Slade. By this time, Opal was awake with the commotion, and asked "What did you say about some rabbits?"

Slade repeated what he had seen, as well as his concerns for their safety. Opal began to worry that maybe some of the rabbits were her relatives and friends from the area.

After some time of carefully deliberating what to do, Slade announced "There is only one solution: we must dig a new tunnel away from the river to an area that is hopefully more safe." Violet added, "But the only route away from the river is toward the road and that red brick building, how can that be safe?" They began to debate what is more secure, going toward or away from the river. Opal began to cry, and Violet said she was worried about where she would have her baby muskrats if the burrow was not available. Mr. Toad suddenly remembered how he had heard some frogs calling to each other down in a storm drain last summer. He and Abbie could hear their amplified voices, making them sound like there were a few dozen frogs down there. The storm drain was under the road and somehow connected the brick building through pipes into the earth. "I think there is another way to safely cross the road to get away from the river," Mr. Toad exclaimed. He explained how he thought the storm drain exited into the hillside close to where the burrow is and how the other end of it went up to the red brick building. "All I would have to do is climb up through this roof to see how far away the storm drain is and then dig down until we find the pipe," he said proudly. "Don't you think that would take a lot of time, toads are not known to dig very fast?" Slade asked impatiently. "Muskrats are efficient tunnelers, just show us where and we can get it done."

Mr. Toad climbed up through the roots and mulch to the surface and took a look around. He didn't see anyone. He lined up the window he and Abbie looked out from to help find where the storm drain was. He counted how many hops it took to get back to where he left the burrow, thankful that Abbie had taught him how to count. Making his way down to the others, Slade asked,"Well, what did you find out?" "From the top of the burrow, it's six-hundred and thirty-six hops," he said with deep satisfaction. "But how far it that?" Slade demanded, having no idea how far a toad's hop is. The four of them stood in the burrow, frustrated and disappointed, having a solution, but not knowing how to access that solution. Suddenly, they heard rain falling over the top of the burrow roof. Not soft gentle rain, but hard, pouring, earth-drenching rain. Mr. Toad thought about how the frogs' croakings were louder after a rainfall, and wondered if that was how they entered the storm drain. He explained to the muskrats and rabbit that maybe all they had to do was find a flow of water from the road into the hillside and that would lead them to the drain system. They agreed it was worth a try, as no one had any other ideas, so using their combined survival senses, the muskrats set off cautiously digging in the direction of the storm drain with Opal and Mr. Toad a safe distance behind. After what seemed like hours, Slade said "I think we have it, I hear a steady stream of water flowing out of a big opening in the earth toward the river and there's more dampness there." He and Violet broke through the earth with a big gush of water splashing onto their faces. They walked up toward the source of the water and found the pipe from the bottom of the drain. They could easily stand up in it, and there were rocks along the sides which were damp, but out of the water for Opal and Mr. Toad.

"Well, we are here, now what do we do?" Violet asked. "I say we stay here until the rain stops, at least we are safely away from the river's edge," Slade said as he lay on his back, resting from his efforts. At least we know the way back to the burrow for food if we have to stay here for awhile. They all agreed as they stared up to the top of the drain through its grates up at the gray sky.

The afternoon brought sunshine and they noticed the level of water at the bottom of the drain had run out into the hillside. They all giggled at how their voices were loud and echoed within the walls of the drain, enabling them to sound like creatures different from muskrats, rabbits and toads. Suddenly, Mr. Toad stopped laughing, his little, keen ears focused on a familiar sound. It was a dog barking, yes…it was Abbie! Oh, to be able to get to the top of the grate and be with her. He could hear her mom talking to another human. Abbie's Shih Tzu friend, Maggie was standing with her as well. Opal said, "What's the matter, you look like you're about to cry!" "That's her, that's her, my friend Abbie I told you about." Quick everybody, make lots of noise so Abbie will look down here and see us!" Mr. Toad said. After a moment of uncertainty, they all made their respective animal noises as loud as they could, pointing their little faces toward the sky. Abbie and Maggie noticed right away, and walked over to the grate, pointing their tiny noses into the grate's openings. Abbie began to bark, aware that there was something unusual going on in the dark down there, but her mom pulled her away from the grate, thinking that her paw might get stuck in it.

After a few minutes, Abbie, Maggie and their humans walked away. Mr. Toad felt hopeless. How could he and his friends get out of this and back to Abbie and Gabe. As the sun slowly moved toward the west, a glint of sunshine reflected off the grate, causing an opening of the shiny pipe above them to become visible. There seemed to be enough rocks and bricks along the wall that they could use as steps up to an opening. Mr. Toad thought how difficult this would be for all of them. The alternative was to go back to the burrow, but then what would they do? After a lengthy discussion of the pros and cons, they decided this was better than risk being skinned alive. They decided that Opal would go first, then Violet, Slade and Mr. Toad last, in case the steps were weakened, he weighed the least and could find better places to grab on while climbing.

It was a very slow process. Opal was afraid her rabbit legs were too long and her arms too short, making her sure she would fall to her death. When she finally reached the opening, Violet started the climb; she had become heavy with her unborn muskrat pups within her and couldn't maneuver herself with any agility at all. She tried not to look down and just listened to Opal's encouragement from the pipe's opening above. After what seemed like an eternity, she finally grabbed the edge of the pipe and pulled herself in, huffing and puffing. Slade went up next, carefully, as he noticed that Violet's efforts and added weight had started to weaken some of the steps. It was then Mr. Toad's turn. He looked up at his friends staring down to the bottom of the drain where he was. He knew this was his only way out so he gathered all his strength, remembering Gabe as the sunlight sparkled at the edge of the pipe above him.

Chapter 11

A New Family

Slade, Violet, Opal and Mr. Toad all rested, while deciding what their next plan would be. It was starting to get dark, so nighttime would be helpful. They all had excellent nocturnal vision so the darkness of the pipes was not a deterrent for them. They decided to walk uphill to where they could smell fresh cool air entering the pipe. Soon they found the pipe was dry and quite wide so they could walk abreast of each other, feeling optimistic. It ended near the grassy surface, and the cover over it could easily be pushed up and away by Slade's strong forearms. The four of them crawled out into the early evening air, realizing that they could touch the big brick building. Looking out over the lawn, they saw the road, the storm-drain grate, the hillside and the river below. Hunger was first noticed by Mr. Toad, so they eagerly rooted around for food, feeling pleased that they had so far been able to lead themselves to safety.

It was surprisingly quiet so close to the building. There were occasional cars and trucks driving down the road, but as long as they stayed away from it, they could not be seen or heard. Mr. Toad knew the way back into the building was the same way he entered it the first time, hopping up the stairs and down the long hall to Abbie's apartment. He planned on spending the night with Slade, Violet and Opal and then going back to the apartment in the morning. He couldn't help thinking that somehow, Gabe had something to do with getting them out of the danger at the river's edge.

Just before dawn, Mr. Toad heard Violet and Slade moving around the grassy area. He opened his eyes to find that there were three baby muskrats nuzzled beneath Violet, while she was cleaning their little bodies with her soft tongue. Slade sat right near them, sheltering them from any cool early morning breezes. "Wow! Where did they come from?" Mr. Toad asked. He didn't remember having seen any muskrat eggs near them when he went to sleep. "What do you mean, where did they come from? They were just born, right out of my body," said Violet. "They are our babies," she proudly said, looking at Slade, who smiled at her and the three baby muskrats who squirmed under her trying to stay warm and fed. "I didn't know…I don't really… know how I came into life, you see, I don't ever remember having a mother," he said sadly.

Opal awakened to see the babies and squealed with joy, saying how cute they were and how much they looked like Slade. Mr. Toad still felt confused, remembering how Abbie had a mom, and wondered how many other creatures had moms. He asked Opal, "What do you mean they look like Slade?" "Well he is their father, so babies look like their mothers or fathers. What's so weird about that?" she asked him. Mr. Toad felt like there were differences among animals that he could not understand, making him feel more distant and incompatible with the others. He somehow felt inadequate because he never knew his parents.

After a few hours, they noticed more traffic on the road, some humans walking their dogs and some of those people who run very fast as though they were being chased, with no one actually chasing them. It seemed puzzling where they all seemed to be going in a hurry. Only the dogs took their time to sniff around and enjoy the outdoors. Slade suggested that the little group move further up the lawn next to an area where the grass mixed with some shrubs, to give them better shelter. They moved slowly now as the babies were not strong enough to walk on their own, and Violet had to carry them one-by-one in her mouth. Opal stayed close by to give them more shelter. Slade started gathering some of the grasses and weeds to bring food back to their new little nest.

Mr. Toad decided he would start to get back into the apartment. First they had to decide what the plan was for the muskrat family and Opal. She now felt like this was her family since so many rabbits had been killed at the river. Would Mr. Toad return, and what would he do when he returned? They decided he would let them know if it was safe for them to return to their tunnels by the river. In the meantime, they were to stay where they are for safety and try not to be noticed. Slade would have to venture away from the building soon for more food. They couldn't risk being found because if all the grass and shrubs were suddenly eaten, someone would be sure to find them. He would have to wait until dark and bring food back to their nest. A water supply was more difficult. They didn't think that there was water near them, so they could only hope for more rain.

Mr. Toad took one more peek at the muskrat babies and had to admit they were cute in their own way. The others wished him luck and he set off around the building to an open doorway that appeared to be safe. It was busier today, there were more men carrying ladders and construction type things down the corridor. Mr. Toad was relieved they were so busy they didn't have time to look down toward the floor and even if they did, men usually were not afraid of toads. He found himself at Abbie's door and squeezed his little body under the door until he was inside. Her mom was still home, but he knew he didn't have to worry if she saw him. After all, she was the one who had bought him his aquarium home. There it was, near the kitchen, right where it had been, just waiting for him. He hopped over and into it, relaxing in its safety and refuge. He fell asleep for awhile, but awoke when he heard Abbie's mom call her saying that he was back in his home. He heard Abbie bark and come running down the stairs to see him. Abbie's mom gave her some big kisses and left for work.

There they were: together again! He was so happy to be back home, he almost forgot to tell her about his recent adventure. She pressed her little nose against his body and snuggled up to him, for about thirty seconds. Then she began scolding him for leaving and being gone for so long. What was he thinking, he left and didn't tell her where he was. He had never seen her so upset, but he was glad to see she had missed him so much.

When Abbie finally finished lecturing him about being gone so long and making some of her tan hair turn white worrying about him, he began to let her know what had happened along the river to his new friends and the other animals.

Chapter 12
The Burrow

"Why are we taking this path to go home? It's much longer," asked Julian. "Because there is too much going on near the road. It's bad enough the humans have been walking through there all day, but they have dropped some kind of white mud that would stick to our feet until it wore off. I'm not willing to get that all over my fur, are you?" replied Soshi. Even though the two rabbits had been good friends and lived together for a long time, they didn't always agree on things. Julian liked having a daily routine and preferred a predictable life, enjoying the comfort and safety of their deep burrow against the warm foundation of the building near the pipes from the geothermal heating system. It really was quite snug and cozy. Soshi enjoyed decorating their little warren with soft vegetation he would find on their daily trips for food and water. Julian would sometimes act like he was annoyed with him, telling Soshi he wasted too much time doing this. But the reality was he appreciated Soshi's sensitivity to detail and empathy to the needs of their neighbors. "Let's just get home the old way… Ugh! Who are you?" Julian asked, bumping into Opal as she was hopping along with her head down munching on fresh greens and wild herbs. "Oh, sorry, I didn't see you there," she said, embarrassed that she hopped right into Julian's broad backside. "I've never seen you here before, where did you come from?" Julian asked suspiciously. "Now, now, it was an accidental meeting, nothing to get upset over," Soshi exclaimed. "Are you new to the neighborhood?" "Well, sort of, I guess, I'm not sure if I can go back to where I was living, it's not very safe down there," Opal said. "What do you mean, it's not safe?" Soshi asked. "You are welcome in our home, I can't even think about a little rabbit like you not having a safe place to live."

Julian stared harshly at Soshi, how could he even consider inviting someone he didn't know into their home, he wondered. Soshi caught his glance, but went on speaking. "What is your name, little one?" "Opal. I was living by the river but just moved up here near this building." "Why don't you join us for a meal, and you can tell us just what this problem is. Maybe we can help," Soshi said. Julian was becoming more furious by the minute. He cherished the protection their pleasant burrow furnished them. Bringing in a stranger could risk their safety; she could tell others about their warren who would want to move in and drive them out, and then they would have to find a new place to live. What could Soshi be thinking about?

"Come with us, Dear," Soshi said to Opal, "you can tell us all about it while we eat." Soshi led the way, with Opal following him. Julian reluctantly walked behind, a safe distance to be sure no one else was with Opal. They entered the opening to the burrow through the base of a shrub with gnarly roots intertwined with one another. Opal and Soshi had no problem wiggling through the opening; Julian's wider body required more effort to squeeze between the root structures. It was annoying to him that Soshi did not want to widen the opening to accommodate his larger size. Soshi felt that a smaller opening would prevent larger animals from getting through the thick roots. Julian knew that Soshi was right, but he complained every time he entered or left the warren. Opal looked around the space that Soshi and Julian called their home and noticed that it was carefully thought out, with the main entrance they had just used at the upper end, and a more narrow exit that was covered with small rocks that could be quickly removed if need be. The walls were covered with fragrant, fresh wild herbs and the sleeping area was made of layers of dried pine needles to keep insects and mold away. She thought about the difference between this warren and that of Violet and Slade's home, that they had so generously shared with her. Surely theirs was much larger, with many more interconnected tunnels under the hillside, but then muskrats were much larger and stronger than rabbits, and there was much more land near the river compared to this space next to the building. It was much warmer and drier; however, it did not have as convenient a water supply.

"Now, my dearest Opal," Soshi said, "please be so kind as to explain what is this danger happening by the river. Julian and I usually stay away from there, we are fortunate to have plenty of food on this side of the road. I don't like crossing that area, too many trucks and cars going through." As they munched on the grasses, rhizomes and flower stems, Opal explained the events of the past few days, the changes in some of the river animals, how she met Mr. Toad, all about Slade and Violet, how they had to escape through the storm drain up to the building, and Violet's new babies. Soshi and Julian listened attentively as Opal described how hungry she was after their escape, and how she was just looking for some food when she accidentally hopped on Julian's soft rump. "I'm so sorry, I hope I didn't hurt you, I just didn't see you there…I wasn't expecting to see anyone there." "Well, you are just lucky it was me, and not a fox. I can tell you don't know much about how to protect yourself," Julian declared pompously. "Now, now, Opal, don't you worry about a thing. Julian and I have many friends up here. I think we can help you." "Please don't go near the river, I wouldn't want anything bad to happen to you," Opal pleaded. "You don't know how bad things are down there. I just wish there was something I could do to warn the others at the river and to somehow change things back to the way they were."

Julian was doubtful about Opal's story, having a difficult time accepting the idea that some animals had been killed and skinned, and many others were acting like they were sick. Opal noticed the way Julian was looking at her, making her feel like an intruder. She said, "I should probably go back now, Slade and Violet will be wondering where I am. I don't want them to worry." "So you aren't planning on staying here with us?" Julian asked, relieved to hear she was about to leave. "Why no, I have friends I live with. And I need to be there in case Violet needs some help with her babies."

Soshi hugged Opal as she turned to climb up through the entrance of the warren. "You are welcome here anytime," he said. "Anything we can do to help out just let us know. Does your friend Violet need more food to take care of those babies? Just let us know where they are and we'll bring some fresh grasses." "Thank you, I think having no water supply could be a problem, there's no river up here," Opal replied. She hurried up the hole and across the underbrush to where Violet and the babies were settled in the deep brush. "Oh Violet, I just met two rabbits who don't live too far from here. One of them said they could help with food if you needed more for yourself to feed the babies." "That's so nice of them. They don't even know me," Violet gushed.

Opal noticed that Violet appeared to look tired and that she had lost some weight. "Slade is out again looking for some water. These babies are always hungry. He said he thought he noticed some different kind of plant shoots that had a lot of water inside of them." It was mid afternoon by now and the baby muskrats were becoming more active and demanding more feedings from Violet. Opal thought about how much her life had changed since meeting Mr. Toad and their journey to find a new home away from the dangers at the river. She thought her new friendship with Soshi was a good indication that maybe this was a good place to call home, even if she wasn't so sure about Julian. She wondered if Mr. Toad had made it back inside the building to Abbie safely.

Chapter 13
Unconditional Love

"We need to talk to Gabe," Abbie said. "I'm not sure exactly how to contact him though." They both sat there together forlornly, in front of the big window overlooking the river. "I heard you call my name." They both looked up and saw a sparkling scintillation of light materialize into their beautiful friend, Gabe. Mr. Toad jumped up for joy, with complete happiness at seeing Gabe again. "I wasn't sure I'd ever see you again," he said. "But you did, remember that sparkle of sunlight at the grate when you were at the bottom of the storm drain?" Gabe asked. "That did remind me of you!" Mr. Toad exclaimed. "I hope you learned your lesson about being too curious. However, there was some purpose in you learning about the abominations going on at the river." Gabe explained the reasons why a human wants to re-engineer life on earth. "This scientist believes he should have won the Watson Genetics Award, which is given to the top scientist who uses his or her discoveries to enhance natural life. Because he didn't receive this award, he was not offered the vice-president of research position at an important biotech corporation. So he decided to use his knowledge to secretly cause many life forms to become mutated and then have the genetic aberrations he caused to happen be 'discovered'. He stands to become very wealthy and influential with some environmental groups and the public because everyone will demand that something be done to stop the mutations."

"This whole thing makes me afraid, like it's much bigger than any toad could ever handle. Why don't the humans know about this?" Mr. Toad asked. "They are better able to stop this than we are." "Because this person, his name is Professor Grimes, is very well known and respected, it would be very difficult right now for humans to believe he would even consider such retaliation on the environment. He makes decisions based on what he wants to do, not what is the right thing to do. He actually organized a global environmental group to raise large sums of money whose goal is supposedly to reduce pollution. You see, he himself is secretly causing the environmental destruction to gain support for his environmental group, that way he can point to the genetic damage he produced himself and make money trying to correct that damage." "Wow! Is that what you meant when you said there is deceit and destruction in the world?" Abbie asked. "Precisely. Someone choosing to use his talents at the expense of destroying the environment," Gabe explained.

Abbie looked at Mr. Toad and noticed the parotid glands on his back seemed more prominent. She had learned that this happened when he became excited, so she said "I don't know about you, but the idea of innocent animals being harmed makes me want to help in any way I can. What do you think?" Mr. Toad was thinking about what he had seen by the river and how he, Opal, Violet and Slade had escaped through the storm drain system. He remembered how seeing the light sparkle through the grate while he was at the bottom of the drain reminded him of Gabe, which gave him the courage to climb to the top, something he probably would not have done if he had let his fears overcome him. "I'm not sure what I can do, but I will try my best to help," he said.

Gabe continued, "There is one power that no amount of confusion or deception can overcome: this power is Unconditional Love." He continued, "This kind of love extends beyond time and space; anything is possible with this pure love. It overcomes the burdens of gravity and the laws of classical physics." "What is physics?" Abbie and Mr. Toad both questioned together. "Physics helps to explain how things in the universe work, but you won't need to learn about it in order to help, because the Creator's power is above the laws of physics and that is what will be enabling you to help. Never forget that."

"First, you need to understand what Unconditional Love really is, because there are many kinds of love. One of the problems is what one person calls love is not always the same as another person's understanding of love. We can say we love our favorite food or pillow, but this is different from the way we love our family." Gabe explained. Abbie thought about this and realized even though she loved her favorite snacks, it was different from the way she loved her mom, which gave her warm, happy feelings inside when her mom held her closely and gave her kisses.

Mr. Toad had to really think about this, because he never knew his mom. Toad mothers just lay hundreds of eggs after the toad father fertilizes them. The eggs are left on their own, some are eaten by predators, others float away, and the lucky ones develop into tadpoles to become toads. This made him feel a little jealous of Abbie, a feeling he recognized he didn't like to have. She and her mom welcomed him into their home and made him part of their family. There was a compromise to this; he didn't have the whole outside world to explore, but he did gain a warm, safe place to live. And, he now realized that he did love Abbie. After having been away from her, he discovered how much he missed her and that her anger with him while he was gone was her way of letting him know how much she loved him, even though he was a toad and she was a dog.

Gabe went on, "Loving our family and friends is easy. But what about those we don't know, or who are different from us, or those who don't even like us, and try to harm or destroy us?" Mr. Toad thought about the snakes, fox, cats and other animals who would like to eat him. He thought, "How could I ever love them?" Gabe knew what he was thinking and said, "There is a natural order to life on Earth, every creature must die someday. But the one thing that doesn't die is the bond of Unconditional Love. The Creator loves us all unconditionally, and wants us to love Him the same way. This bond of Unconditional Love is Pure Love and is what keeps us connected to the Creator so we can make bonds of Pure Love with others. Pure love cannot die, because it is the life force of Creation and is what keeps us connected to loved ones after death. That is why deceit and hatefulness lead to destruction and death: they are the opposite of love."

Abbie thought about what it would be like to not be with her mom every day and she could not imagine not waking up in bed, getting cuddled and groomed, and all the other things that were part of her daily routine. She knew her mom loved her very much because she had promised her she would never let her suffer. She felt that her life was complete and totally safe when she was with her mom, and realized she and her mom had this bond of pure love between them. Sometimes her mom would cry when she thought about them not being together.

"So does this mean we have to love this Professor Grimes person?" Abbie wondered aloud. "When we see someone who is so determined to destroy natural life, we have to be careful we don't become hateful and vengeful ourselves. Those kinds of feelings become entangled with confusion, deceit and destruction. It's better to focus on the right reasons to stop this evil, to bring others together for the mutual benefits of everyone. Now this isn't always an easy thing to do, because there is so much diversity in the natural world, but this is part of the Creator's Plan. By working together, even with differences of opinion, obstacles can be overcome by respecting one another, following the Natural Laws, and recognizing the right to life for everyone. We must still treat others the way we want to be treated ourselves, even with others who do not share our beliefs and values, it's that simple. That is the message."

Abbie was still thinking about the bond of love and about loving others. "I don't see how loving others would make me love them the way I love my mom,"she said. "You wouldn't. That forever love bond only happens when two creatures willingly make the choice to love each other in a special way forever, no matter what. When we live a loving life, that is to respect and understand others the way we want to be understood and respected, it promotes peace and harmony in the world according to the Creator's Plan, but that is different from 'forever love'. I'm glad you asked that question, it's important to understand how these two kinds of love are different. Now, there are people in the world who choose not to work together to improve life, but to destroy it. As long as we choose to not become destructive and deceitful ourselves, we are following the Creator's Plan for our own purpose in life," Gabe said.

Mr. Toad was still ruminating about caring for an animal which was his natural predator, he couldn't seem to get past those thoughts. Gabe, as usual, knew what he was thinking. "No matter who we are, big or small, weak or powerful, we are all creatures of the Creator. Accepting who we are is the first step. Because you are an amphibian, how you normally think is different from, let's say, mammals, like Abbie. If you just remember you are loved by the Creator and not become frozen with fear, you will start to understand how you fit into His Plan to help make the world more peaceful and harmonious."

Chapter 14

Meta-Physics

"So how do we go about helping? I can't fit through small cracks like a toad. And my mom will surely notice if I'm not here. We are very close you know," she said looking up to Gabe through her long lashes, with her pig tails hovering over her eyes. "Getting you out of here won't be a problem, neither will the time you will be gone. You see, the time and space thing are part of the crystal that you see me appear from. This dimension of the visible world is part of the crystal too, but you don't need to know all about that. It's part of a special kind of Physics, but don't worry you don't have to know how it works to be a part of it," Gabe said. "Are you ready? Mr. Toad, jump on Abbie's back, and Abbie, I'll put you on my shoulder and we'll go." They both did as Gabe told them, and before they knew what was happening, they were part of the sparkling light themselves, feeling weightless and connected with something wonderful like they had never before experienced.

Chapter 15

Just Dropping In

Abbie and Mr. Toad found themselves alone standing near the entrance of Soshi and Julian's warren. "Where are we?" Abbie asked. "I think we are near the back of the building by the looks, the sounds and the smells," the toad answered. Just then, Abbie thought she saw something furry pop out of the ground, only to dive back in just as quickly. She excitedly pounced over the spot to investigate, pressing her nose into the hole. It smelled warm and like a mammal. She wasn't sure what kind of mammal, but knew it was still in the hole because it had a very fresh scent. She could hear someone arguing down the hole but couldn't make out what was being said. She barked to let whoever was down there know she was there. Mr. Toad hopped over to take a look as well.

"I told you not to let anyone know about our home, that they would want to chase us out so they could move in," Julian said. He could hear Abbie digging at the top of the hole to get more information about what and who was down there. "Calm down, calm down! Getting so nervous won't do a thing," Soshi said, trying to soothe Julian's emotions. Just then, Mr. Toad rolled down the opening that Abbie had enlarged from her digging. "Who are you?" Julian shouted at Mr. Toad. He was surprised, but relieved to see it was only a toad, nothing to be afraid of. "Well... well! What's your name?" Soshi asked. Before Mr. Toad could say a word, Abbie slid down the opening almost on top of him. He jumped out of the way to avoid getting squashed. The two rabbits stood next to each other with their ears pointed straight up and their mouths open.

A dog had never been in their home. They had seen dogs before, attached to a human by a leash, as they walked or ran along. None of that ever made sense to a rabbit; why would they let themselves be led around like that? No wonder they barked. Rabbits were nice and quiet, and could hop around whenever and wherever they wanted. Abbie sneezed, to get the dirt out of her tiny nose, spreading the wet spray all over them. They all stood there in silence for a moment each one trying to understand what just happened. Julian was still in shock with the unexpected arrivals and too flabbergasted to speak. "Excuse me, but eh, may I ask what made you ah, drop in?" Soshi asked Abbie. "I'm sorry, I didn't think I would have come in with such a crash, I mean I wasn't trying to fall down, I guess gravity just got me going and then, well, here I am," she said. She could tell the two rabbits were fearful of her, which was a surprise because there were not many animals that were afraid of her. She was just a small dog, after all. She noticed that one of the rabbits was about the same size as her, and realized that was why the opening was big enough for her to fit through so easily. She had not expected to tumble down face first, thinking the bows on her pigtails must be full of dirt. Sand continued to fall into her eyes when she moved her head, causing her to give out another big sneeze toward all of them.

Soshi recovered from the shock of having a dog in the warren before Julian, who continued to stare speechlessly at Abbie. "What do you want from us?" he asked. Abbie and Mr. Toad started to speak at the same time; "We just sort of arrived at the top of the hole in the ground that leads here." Mr. Toad had more experience venturing down holes in the ground than Abbie, who only occasionally would scratch the surface of the earth if she found an insect crawling around. She usually had no interest in digging like some dogs do. She was a little embarrassed with the ordeal and didn't like being in a dark and sandy underground space. In fact, it was something she had never even conceived could exist. The contrast between being with Gabe in sparkling light a few moments earlier and now in a dark damp hole seemed unimaginable. "We were brought here by a… ummm, friend of ours. He sort of, you know, just dropped us off at the surface of your ummm… home," Mr. Toad replied, trying to not look too foolish. "And just who is this friend of yours? What are your names and why are you here?" Julian asked loudly, having recovered his speech. "My name is Abbie, and I really like bunnies, I always have," she said. "I'm sure you do, lots of animals like to eat bunnies, as you say," Julian retorted. "Oh, that's not what I meant at all. I mean I like the way they smell and hop around. I've seen lots of bunnies where I have lived," she said. Julian glared at her suspiciously. Soshi inquired, "Were you looking for someone?" he asked politely. "My name is Mr. Toad, I have a good friend Opal, who is a bunny, I mean a rabbit," he replied. "Would you happen to know where she is? I think she lives close by. She's new to this area though." Soshi answered, "She was here a little while ago, such a sweet little rabbit, but she is gone now." "You see, it's important we find her, I think that's why we were, ahhhh, dropped off above your home here," the toad explained. "Well, if you are a friend of Opal's that puts a different perspective on things," Soshi said. "Do you know where she is?" the toad asked. "She didn't say where she is living, but said something about needing to get back to her friend Violet and her babies." Soshi answered.

Chapter 16

A Dark Plan

"Did anyone see you coming into the building?" Professor Grimes asked Juice. Since his usual mood was one of impatience and intolerance, his voice always sounded angry, even when he tried to speak in a hushed tone. "Yes, yes, I did like you said. No one was around, I checked," Juice replied. "You came by the security cameras I told you to walk by, right?" Grimes had hacked into the digital security system on his laptop and methodically shut off the cameras that Juice would be passing on the way up to the old laboratory. It was important that only one camera at a time would be off-line for a few seconds to prevent the system from detecting a problem.

The old lab was dusty and dimly lit to prevent the escape of light. If the room were normally illuminated, the light would have cast a glow through the translucent fiberglass panels.

Professor Grimes looked at Juice, thinking he had chosen him well. He was a very tall, powerfully built man, capable of the physical strength to carry heavy containers of chemicals and tools needed for his plan. However, his intellectual prowess was considerably less impressive than his physique. He tended to be impulsive and took great pleasure in intimidating anyone or anything smaller or weaker than he was. He viewed himself as superior to others because of his Herculean size and liked to bully others and mercilessly kill small animals just for his own amusement. That was why he enjoyed skinning animals so much. Looking into a terrified rabbit, beaver or raccoon's eyes while he skinned them alive made him feel powerful. It was also the reason Grimes' project appealed to him so much. He could be the brawn behind an environmental movement that would change the world, even though he didn't understand any of the science behind the plan. What appealed to him was the power and scale of the plan and the potential for riches.

Professor Grimes smirked at Juice. "We're getting close to the most important phase in this mission. What we've done so far has just been a test which has produced results far more impressive than I ever imagined. The few biological life cycles I have seen prove that I can actually change the genetics and appearance of various lifeforms. You have no idea what this means. Since I know how to cause the genetic damage, I will be the one to tell the world what the damage is and what can be done to control more environmental damage. Of course, no one will know that it was I who caused the damage. Once people see how grotesque cute little animals become, and how big and aggressive insects have become, and how vegetation will change, they will be begging me to help them correct the problems. People will recognize the potential for their own genetic mutations, and they will be willing to pay anything to prevent that from happening. This is so much better than I had ever hoped for." He couldn't control his chuckling, which erupted into a roar of laughter, which surprised even Juice. "The economic and environmental impact this will have will be enormous. There will be corporations who will give me thousands of shares of their stocks for my knowledge."

"What about us though?" Juice asked. Could those things happen to us and we become, well, weird and ugly?" Juice was thinking about his body becoming misshapen or weakened. "Yes, it would affect us too if we are not careful. That's why I always tell you to wear the gloves and other protective clothing I give you. Right now, our only risk is being bitten by one of the affected insects, like a mosquito. We will be wearing insect repellent, long sleeved shirts, hats and boots to protect ourselves. We're not about to drink any of the water from the river or catch a fish and eat it. We won't be spending much more time around here after we complete Phase 2 of the project. I will be organizing a little kayaking trip with my environmental group to take some "samples" of the water for publicity purposes, just to get things going. The others in the group will notice some of the changes and ask me to examine the specimens. That's when the whole environmental thing will take off like an erupting volcano!"

"Let's go over the schedule again. I want to be sure you know what to do and in what order. After tonight we'll be communicating mostly by phone. Now that you know how to enter the building as I disable the security system, you can get in and out of the lab as I tell you what I need. I don't want to take any chances being seen. Nobody knows who you are, so even if you are seen by residents or the construction crew, they'll think you belong here."

There was something Grimes said that started to make Juice feel uncomfortable. He didn't care about the purpose of the "project", but he did care about being caught on camera, and of having more exposure entering and leaving the tower. He felt like Grimes' plan was to put him in the riskiest part of the project, while he would be away from the dangers, promoting his environmentalist program. He thought he deserved more money because of this, and decided he would wait until the proper time and demand his salary be doubled. After all, he reasoned, if he was doing all the work, he should be paid more for his time and talents.

<h2 style="text-align:center">Chapter 17</h2>

And Passing Through

Julian glared at Abbie, still in disbelief that a dog had entered their home, uninvited, face first. "Excuse me," he protested. "You have disturbed our home, what would it take for you to leave here as soon as possible? What do you need to get out of here?" he asked, scowling at Abbie. "Um, I'm not sure, I've never been so deep in the ground before," she said. "Now, now, don't worry about a thing, we do have another entrance that isn't so steeply inclined," Soshi exclaimed. "It will take a little longer, it's not so direct, but has a much gentler slope to the surface that I think will be better suited for you, Abbie dear."

They agreed to try this other exit from the warren, with Soshi leading. Julian remained behind, vowing to never let another dog into his cozy home. Mr. Toad had hopped onto Abbie's back, as Soshi and Abbie could cover more ground much quicker than he could springing along on his own. Abbie's eyes eventually adjusted to the darkness, but with the sand in her little nose and bumping into Soshi's fluffy cottontail, she kept sneezing as the trio made their way toward the surface. It seemed like there was a downward slope in the tunnel to Abbie. How could they be coming to the surface if they were trending down. She thought maybe she lost her sense of direction, with no light, no sounds and her constant sniffling and sneezing. What was happening to her? She was making some soft whimpers that Mr. Toad heard and felt through her back as he held on to her coat with his tiny little fingers. "It's all right, don't be scared," he reassured her.

By now he could tell she was feeling uneasy with the whole ordeal. "Just think of Gabe up there, he wouldn't have sent us down here if it wasn't safe," he said, trying to sound optimistic. They noticed the soil was becoming damp and the tunnel had started to smell musty. It made Abbie sneeze more forcefully now and her eyes had started to tear up as well. Mr. Toad suddenly noticed the scents within the tunnel and immediately recognized there were very near the river. Soshi picked up more speed now as the angle of the slope had become very steep now, his back legs splashing water in Abbie's little face.

They noticed there was light ahead through what looked like a thick green curtain. Abbie stopped short, almost catapulting Mr. Toad off her back. He grabbed one of her pigtails and held on for dear life, remaining perched on top of her round head. He feared landing under the powerful hind legs of the rabbit and grimaced at the thought of what would be left of his tiny body. "Why did you stop?" he asked her, panting heavily. "I don't know, something just made me stop. I don't know if it's because of my sneezing or my eyes all watery, but I had to stop," she said, almost in disbelief.

They noticed that Soshi had sprung through the green curtain, which turned out to be thick weeds near the river's edge. They could hear the water flowing by. Abbie had been to the river before with her mom, and had no interest in standing on the ground, preferring to view the river from the safety and comfort of her pink stroller. Mr.

Toad jumped off her shoulders and the two of them peered through the tall grass at the end of the tunnel trying to find Soshi. They saw him a few feet away where the water just met the land, hungrily chewing on some very thick weeds that had some dark brown spots on the stalks. The two of them looked at one another and remembered Gabe's words about focusing on being part of the Creator's plan and not on one's fears. They noticed that as Soshi chewed on the stalks, the brown spots dissolved into brown liquid that stained the fur around his mouth. He noticed them at the end of the tunnel and called out to them to join him, saying the weeds tasted much better today than usual and they should join him in his little snack. Abbie and Mr. Toad looked at one another again, both glad that weeds were not part of their diets.

"Where do we go from here?" Abbie asked Soshi as he continued to munch on the stalks. "Wherever you would like, this is the end of the tunnel, you are out and in the open air. It's all flat ground now." They looked up at the sky above them and then back to the river, and noticed a bright sparkle of light ahead of them and decided to follow it. Abbie considered taking a drink of water from the river, but decided against doing so, as did Mr. Toad. They waved a thank you and good-bye to Soshi who was still munching on the tall green stalks at the river's edge.

Chapter 18
A Masked Myrtle

"We should try to avoid being seen," Mr. Toad told Abbie. It's easy for me, but since you are a dog, you are likely to scare some animals off." "Don't be silly. I agree we should avoid being seen, but there are animals here big enough to eat me too. There are fox and birds of prey and snakes and coyotes and…" "Will you stop that? How do you know about this, you hardly ever left the apartment?" he asked testily. "My mom would tell me about all the things that could hurt me and how she would always protect me from them," Abbie explained, "except she is not here to protect me now. I wonder what she is doing, and if she misses me yet." "Don't you remember what Gabe said, the whole time-space thing with the crystal, we won't be missed because of that. Besides, if your mom ever saw you now, she wouldn't even recognize you because you don't look like a Shih Tzu, being all wet and dirty. You kind of look wild, like you blend right in along the river." He had to laugh as he looked and noticed the bows holding her pigtails had fallen off and her hair was in her eyes like a dirty stray dog.

Mr. Toad decided to hop on Abbie's back again to get a better view of what lay ahead, not that he was very high off the ground, since her legs were not very long, but it provided a better vantage point and they could talk more easily as they walked along. Suddenly Abbie found herself eye to eye, staring into a masked face with a fish in its mouth. The face growled loudly at her and tried to push her head away, almost knocking Mr. Toad off her shoulders. She gave out a soft cry, startled at the sight. The masked face stared at her eyes and saw the confusion, and realized she did not pose a threat. The face dropped the fish on the ground and said, "Who are you, and how did you get so lost?" "My name is Abbie and this is my very best friend, Mr. Toad. We're uh, traveling together. What's your name, and why are you wearing a mask?" "What mask are you talking about? What's wrong with you? Haven't you ever seen a raccoon before? My name is Myrtle. I was just about to have some dinner I just caught. It doesn't get any fresher than this," she smiled at the wriggling fish.

"I usually don't talk with dogs, so many of them just want to chase me down, and they don't stop until I scratch their eyes with my long nails. I am very proud of my hands you know, raccoons are known to be very smart and dexterous. We can figure out almost anything and usually get what we want," Myrtle replied, with a self-confident smile. "Yes, I can see what you mean," Abbie said, scrutinizing her well-manicured hands. "We're not here to interfere with your dinner, just passing through that's all. "What brought you down here? I'm curious," Myrtle asked. "Actually, we aren't really sure, but we're here to stop some bad things that are happening to the environment at the river," Abbie explained. "What kinds of things?" Myrtle's eyes narrowed, making Abbie think she was about to scratch her eyes out, making her step back a little. She wasn't sure what else to say, when she noticed the bright sparkles of light a few feet behind the raccoon. Abbie remembered Gabe's words about not letting fear get in the way of respecting life, giving her the courage to continue. "Well, if you would like, we could tell you more about our purpose of being here," Abbie said. Myrtle relaxed a little, making Abbie and Mr. Toad realize that she didn't really have a mask across her face at all, it was just part of the darker bands of fur that ran across her back and through her long bushy tail. "That sounds like a plan," Myrtle said, "but let's get away from here first. I don't like being out in the open for very long. Follow me."

Mr. Toad hopped onto Abbie's back again and the three of them walked away from the river. He was surprised how slowly raccoons walked, waddling from side to side. He wasn't sure if it was because Myrtle still had the fish in her mouth or she always walked like that because she had so much fur on her body. He decided he would not ask right now, thinking he should not do anything to upset her. She seemed like she could become vicious at any minute. He thought Abbie was being brave following so closely behind the raccoon. His thoughts wandered to Violet, Slade and the babies, wondering if they were still safe in their new home against the building. Myrtle led them to a hollowed out tree and started the climb toward her nest near the top, using the claws on her front and hind paws very efficiently. Abbie stopped short at the base of the tree, calling out to Myrtle, "Hey, hold on, I can't climb you know, I can't follow you up there. Can we go somewhere else to talk?"

Chapter 19
Water Works

"Violet, Slade and the babies had settled in to their new home. It was not as spacious as what they had under the big oak tree overlooking the river, but it was easier to get in and out of, something which proved to be convenient for the new family. Opal spent most of her time there, playing with the babies and keeping Violet company. They had become good friends by now. She left to help Slade find food for his family and for herself. She discovered that there were certain times every day when all of a sudden water would begin to spray out of the ground at various places, watering the grass and other plants growing near the building. This proved to be a stroke of luck for her and Slade. He decided he could divert some of the water into a small rivulet if he dug a few inches into the soil, thereby providing a supply of fresh water for his family close to their new home. It wouldn't be a constant supply of water, but it was clean and solved the problem of where they would find water. The babies were almost big enough to start venturing out of the nest to play in the mud. They noticed the water supply would come on twice a day, providing more water than they needed. "I think it's a little too soggy now with all this extra water," he said to Opal. "I think I'm going to dig another little trench to divert some of the water away from the nest, what do you think? I can always change it back if it becomes too dry." "I can help if you want me to, or else I can bring what we just gathered back to the nest." "Why don't you do that, I can manage this by myself, besides I dig much faster than you can." He thought how much Opal had really become part of the family now, even though she was not a muskrat. They had all learned to use the skills each of them had to improve all of their lives. Slade worked quickly, wanting to block off and redirect the trench away from the nest before the water started to flow again.

Chapter 20
River Rumors

Myrtle sighed heavily hearing Abbie's complaint that she couldn't climb up through the hollow in the old tree. "What good are dogs anyway, they can't climb, they have no thumbs, they can't fish or open up things which might have food inside," she thought to herself. She let go of the fish she had been carrying in her mouth, and started back down to the ground where Abbie and Mr. Toad were waiting. "OK, OK, I have plan B then. Let's go to another place to talk. It's a small shack I go into sometimes in the winter. There's some stuff in there which makes some soft noises which keeps it warm if you don't mind that." She led the way up a slight incline toward a small building. Abbie and Mr. Toad, who were familiar with structures humans had built, noticed it had a door that looked like it was securely shut. It proved to be no challenge for Myrtle as she reached up with her little hand-like paws, and turned the knob. The door swung open and the trio walked in. There was a little bench which looked like someone had placed it there just for their purpose to sit and talk together. Abbie and Mr. Toad were amazed at Myrtle's dexterity in opening the door, feeling inferior to the raccoon for the first time. Mr. Toad gulped, imagining what her perfect little hands could do to him if she wanted to harm him. Myrtle glared back at them, saying, "There, now does this meet your needs?" Abbie looked up, reading the words printed on the wall of the shed. "Fire Sprinkler System Pump and Switch Panel: Read Directions before using," she read aloud. The raccoon snapped her head around to where Abbie's gaze was focused and then back at Abbie. "What are you saying?" she asked Abbie. "I'm just reading what those words are on the wall. That's what this stuff is for in this shed, something to do with a fire system, probably for the building I live in up on the hill." Myrtle was amazed that those marks on the wall actually said something. She had no idea that marks that looked like scratches could have a meaning. She thought to herself that maybe dogs had some skills after all. "You live up in that big red building? I've never been in there, although I have tried to get in. I think it is raccoon-proof."

"So tell me, why are you both here?" Myrtle asked, feeling somewhat humbled by Abbie's literacy. "Well, have you noticed anything peculiar around the river?" Mr. Toad queried, having seen and heard for himself some of the horrors there. "I've noticed there have been more animals dying. There is one area where so many carcasses have washed up on the shore that the smell is awful, I won't go anywhere near there. Raccoons have a very keen sense of smell you know." Abbie glanced at Mr. Toad, rolling her eyes about Myrtle's latest boastfulness about the superior traits of raccoons. "I have to fish upriver to avoid the smell. I have also come across some animals which had been skinned, all their fur is gone. Muskrats, fox, rabbits, beavers and even raccoons. Just left dead there on the ground. Usually birds like crows or falcons will swoop down and eat the remains, but for some reason, no one wants them, they just stay there, rotting with bugs all over them. It's a terrible sight. Those of us who have been there can't even recognize if some of the bodies are our family members or friends. With no fur, it's just about impossible to tell who they were. Mr. Toad and Abbie realized the destruction was much worse than they had thought and began explaining the purpose of their mission to Myrtle. They were glad they had a comfortable place to spend the night, knowing it would be important to have Myrtle included in their plans.

Chapter 21
The Flood

Julian was pacing back and forth in his hutch, waiting for Soshi to return from taking Abbie and Mr. Toad out of the warren through the other lower entrance. He felt vulnerable and alone, especially now that he could still smell the scent of a dog in his home. He was thinking about going down the tunnel himself to find Soshi, when he heard a soft trickle of water running down from the opening of the warren. "Now what?" he asked himself out loud. "First dogs and toads in here, now water!" He looked up and noticed the trickle had turned into a steady stream, eroding the walls of the opening so that the edges had begun to collapse, letting light into the dark space. He jumped up and started to climb out, afraid the space would become a little underground pond. He reached the top with his face, hands and feet covered in mud. The entire grassy area was being sprayed with water which was channeled directly into the warren. "How did this happen?" he snarled to himself. What would he do now? He didn't know where Soshi was, couldn't get back into his home with all this water flowing into it, and couldn't even go down the tunnel to find Soshi now. Where was he going to spend the night? He blamed all of this on the dog and toad, figuring they must have had something to do with his recent bad luck. He warily hopped around the area to investigate what had changed with the topography when he noticed a large muskrat digging in the mud about 100 feet away.

Julian angrily hopped toward the muskrat who seemed to be directing the water toward where he had been standing. "Hey, you! What do you think you are doing?" he demanded of the muskrat. Slade casually looked up at him, noticing the rabbit was quite enraged. "I'm just taking care of my family. What is it to you?" he asked. Julian stomped over until he was face to face with Slade. "I'll tell you what; you are destroying my home, that's what." Just then, Opal appeared, looking surprised at Julian standing there arguing with Slade. "What are YOU doing here?" Julian asked her. "I live here. I told you I was staying with a muskrat family now. Why are you so upset?" "I don't know where

Soshi is. He went down the tunnel to the river to take a toad and dog out of the warren after they both fell down the hole, and he hasn't come back yet. Then if that's not bad enough, I get flooded out of my own home. I followed where the water was coming from and I find this muskrat playing in the mud" Julian explained, feeling relieved to see Opal's familiar face. "Did you say a toad and dog were in your home with Soshi?" Opal asked in amazement. Slade and Opal looked at each other, each smiling broadly. A toad with a dog must be Mr. Toad, they both knew, pleased that he had made it back to his home inside the building and was safe. "Where did you say the toad and dog are now?" Slade asked. "I don't know and I don't care where they are. They said they were 'dropped off' by someone, they didn't say who, but they were looking for you Opal, and I guess you too," referring to Slade. "I have to find Soshi, this is not like him to be away so long."

Opal and Slade glanced at one another, both thinking about the dangers that could have befallen the rabbit. "Look, I can see you are quite upset. I didn't intend to flood your home while I was trying to keep mine nice and dry," Slade said to Julian. "I tell you what, why don't you come stay with us until things settle down for you. What's one more. We have plenty of room." Julian was shocked that a complete stranger would make such a gracious offer to him. Slade's hospitality reminded him of Soshi, who would often display kindness and concern for other animals he did not even know. "Well, if you really don't mind, I guess I could spend the night," Julian reluctantly replied. "Yippee!!" cried Opal, jumping up and down at the thought of spending time with another rabbit, even if it was Julian. "Come this way, I'll introduce you to my little family," Slade said, shuffling along the building toward his nest. Julian followed downheartedly, with Opal hopping energetically behind him.

Chapter 22
The Letter G

"OK, you know where the two dams are, right? I've shown you three times already, you should remember by now. Then there is the hydroelectric plant between the two dams. No one is there at night so that is where you are going to spend most of your time distributing the chemicals in the water. It's a place where industrial materials and supplies are already there, so no one will notice a few more barrels and containers. Besides, I have tripled the concentration of the formula so it can be stored in the smaller containers. That makes it a little heavier to carry and more dangerous, but as long as you follow my instructions, it should not be a problem for you. Remember, always wear the special gloves, mask and eye protection I gave you and you will be fine. I am using the same containers that the hydro plant uses for its generator supplies. I copied the labels so they look identical to the ones they use," Grimes explained. He and Juice were meeting in the lab in the early morning hours to reduce chances of being seen. "How am I going to tell the difference, I mean, which containers are theirs and which ones are ours?" Juice asked. "What's wrong with you?" Grimes screamed at Juice. "Don't you retain anything I have taught you? Sometimes I wonder if I made a big mistake hiring you for this job. I knew I should have looked for someone else who knew how to listen and appreciate the magnitude and importance of this project."

Juice felt his anger and resentment boil up within himself. He asked himself why he had not backed out a few weeks ago, when he first had some reservations about working for Grimes. "When this is completed in a few more days, I'll be glad I won't have to put up with you anymore. You are lame-brained and incapable of learning," Grimes shouted at him. Juice glared back at Grimes, wishing he could just walk out the door and never see Grimes again. But if he left now, he knew he wouldn't get his pay for the week, and he needed the money for his own little projects. "I have marked each of my containers with the letter 'G', in the upper corner, which can only be seen when you shine an ultraviolet light on it. Then it will be visible, even to you," Grimes growled at Juice. "Do you still have the little UV flashlights I gave to you?" "Yes," Juice replied through his clenched teeth. "Good. Don't lose them because you won't be able to tell the difference between my containers and those that are used by the hydro plant. It's essential that everything looks like it's supposed to be there. So when you start bringing the containers there and put them where I told you to, no one will notice they don't contain the lubricants for the generators. Now, let's go through this one more time. Step by step. Tell me, in detail, each phase of your job," Grimes said. He had calmed down by now, pressing his hands over his forehead at the start of another intense headache. Juice thought that by the end of the project, he will have shown Grimes just how smart he really was.

Chapter 23

The Odyssey Flight

Abbie was the first to awaken, which surprised even herself, as she is not usually an early riser. She couldn't get comfortable sleeping on the rough wooden floor of the shed and her immediate thoughts were centered on the vivid dream she had during the night. Trying to recollect the dream, what stood out the most was she and Mr. Toad looking down from some vantage point that was very high, way above tree height. He was standing on her back at the base of her neck, holding onto her pigtails. It seemed like they were flying very quickly but there was no noise of wings beating the air, just the feeling of cool air rushing by their faces. He was perched on her back, like he had been in the tunnel. Only this time their movement came from another source she could not identify. Every so often they would swoop down lower to give them a closer look of what was happening on the ground. They saw various animals living on the ground and birds flying and fish swimming in the river. There were insects crawling, grasses, vines and trees softy swaying in gentle breezes. They then climbed back up to an even higher altitude so all they could see was the meandering river making its way toward the bay and eventually into the ocean. Abbie and Mr. Toad didn't have to speak in the dream, they just knew what the other was thinking. It all looked so beautiful and peaceful they thought to each other.

Suddenly, their direction turned back, with a fast, steep dive, again following the course of the river. This time what they saw was not tranquility but a change in the number and appearance of the animals, fish and insects. Birds were unable to fly because their wings were too small. Fish were dying on the shore. There were squirrels, chipmunks, rabbits, muskrats, beavers and raccoons who had either grown too large to walk on their legs or whose legs were too small and weak to allow them to walk. Insects had grown to be very large, almost the size of sparrows. Grasses, shrubs and underbrush were so thick that even humans were having a difficult time walking to the river. Their roots had grown so far into the river they had blocked the flow, causing it to flood the banks. Much of the vegetation had turned brown, rotting on the stagnant, flooded riverbank. Beavers were desperately trying to redirect the water by engineering their own dams, but seemed to be too weak to cut branches and drag them where they were needed.

The next thing she knew, they were moving away from the river, far away from the big red brick building, flying over the ocean toward a large private yacht with a flag fluttering at its stern. The background of the flag was white, with the earth in green and over the earth was embroidered two hands gripped together in gold. The people on the yacht were talking about what could be done to protect humans from the same devastation that was happening to the lifeforms on the river. They all agreed if they planned things carefully, not only could they overcome the biological disaster, but this would become a vast new source of income for them.

Abbie and Mr. Toad's odyssey flight then brought them back over the river, looking like it usually does. They was a man sitting on a big rock with a fishing rod next to him. He looked up at them, smiled and waved as though he knew them. He was dressed in shabby, old clothes but there seemed to be sunlight shining only on him. There was a group of humans in kayaks, paddling up the river. They wore shirts and hats that had the same symbol the flag on the yacht had. That was when Abbie awoke, looking around her seeing Mr. Toad by her side and Myrtle curled up on the bench.

Abbie turned her head to give Mr. Toad a little lick over his nose. She had to be careful not to press her tongue too hard, he didn't like that. His bulgy eyes snapped open, saying "Whhat, What are you doing, trying to drown me?" "Not at all sleepy head, you're so cute when you sleep, making little toady snoring sounds." "I'm starving, what are we going to eat for breakfast?" he asked. "Me too, but we have to be careful what we eat." She told him about her dream and they both agreed it was a warning from Gabe about what was about to happen to the river environment.

Their voices had awakened Myrtle so she carefully listened to Abbie's descriptions of the destruction she saw in her dream. "Excuse me, but are you saying this was a dream you had? Because I have seen what looks like the beginning of what your dream was about." "We were just saying the thought of breakfast sounds good but we're not sure what is safe to eat anymore. I sure don't want to eat any of those insects affected with that stuff," Mr. Toad anxiously explained. "I'm pretty sure for you, there are some insects that have never left this shed, there is so much here for them to eat. If you just dig down a little bit, you'll find a hearty breakfast for yourself," Myrtle said. "Now for you and I, that is another matter", she said to Abbie. "Since we don't eat bugs, and it's no longer safe for sushi, I will have to round up some food for us. There is a dumpster not far from here, I always find all kinds of human food in there." "You mean, you actually eat food that the humans have thrown away? Like, like... GARBAGE?" Abbie could not believe her ears, how could anyone even think about eating food that people had thrown away. "Not to worry Your Majesty, I will find something that you will like. There is a pizza place that throws out what they don't sell at the end of the day. I eat it all the time. We'll just have to wait until night time though. First of all, I like to sleep most of the daylight, and second, no one will see me going into the dumpster at night. So if you don't mind, I'm going to curl up here and sleep away the day. I'll do the pizza run tonight. But while you were both sleeping last night, I went out to some nearby trash cans and brought back some food that is good for raccoons and dogs. We are genetically related I think, although many DNA mutations ago." Myrtle pulled out some plastic bags that contained moldy bread and soft, mushy bananas. Abbie thanked Myrtle for her thoughtfulness but said she was suddenly not hungry. Mr. Toad took Myrtle's advice and was scooping up varieties of new insects he had never before tasted.

Chapter 24
The Coyotes

Grimes arose before dawn. He needed to check on what he considered his "in vivo" experiment. He had purchased an old farm several years ago with the intention of using the property for animal experiments. Its location was remote, with no other farms or houses nearby. The road to the barn was almost a mile in from the town road. There was no electricity on the property; well water was the only amenity. He drove in toward the barn with a large tub of various cuts of meat which had exceeded their expiration dates for sale at a market. He opened the barn door to be greeted by eight coyotes, who had already smelled the meat in the tubs. They were contained in one of two separate areas in the barn, where either he or Juice would move the pack for feeding and cleaning their area. He was proud of these creatures; they had grown much larger and more powerful than their natural size. They were being given Grimes' "special formula" in their water every day for the past year. He wasn't sure what he was going to do with them eventually. They were obviously more vicious and aggressive than he had ever seen them before. Probably just leave them for Juice to skin, he thought. He threw the raw meat onto the floor at the coyotes as they ravaged every piece. He chuckled and left the barn, whistling to himself and drove back home.

Chapter 25
Caged Prey

Soshi awoke with a headache, feeling dizzy with blurry vision. He did not think he could even stand up, never mind hop back into the tunnel up to his warren. He was confused at why he was even at the river. He eventually remembered it was to lead the toad and dog out of the warren because the dog was not able to climb out. How silly is that, he thought to himself. He tried to stand up again but was unable and fell back down. He thought about Julian and what he was doing. Probably pacing back and forth, waiting for him to return. He realized until he felt better he would have to stay where he was. He wasn't hungry anyway. The thought of eating more of the grass stalks he had yesterday made him feel queasy. He was about to close his eyes when he heard footsteps moving toward him. The ground shook a little from them. He looked up to find a large man wearing big leather gloves, grinning at him. Soshi quivered, unable to run away. The man picked him up by the ears and roughly tossed him into a wire cage. He laughed, saying something like he would be easy to skin, spat out a large wog of tobacco onto the ground next to the cage and walked on. Soshi found himself next to a young raccoon and a mink, both shaking in fear. Their eyes all met, causing them to shiver in unison. The big man sat on a log overlooking the river, drinking something hot and brown from a green and white cup.   He ate several pieces of food wrapped in plastic and when he was done, he threw everything on the ground and left it there. He took some rectangular object out of his pocket and started talking to it as though someone was with him. Soshi and the others could hear another human voice coming out of the object. They couldn't understand what was being said, but the voice coming out of the rectangular object sounded loud and angry. The big man put the object back into his pocket and said some words that seemed to be very hateful.

The large man picked up the cage with Soshi, the mink and the young raccoon and carried it near the base of a very large tree. He left them there, walking toward the river. He felt powerful, dressed in a new camo hunting outfit with a large knife sheathed on his belt and wore the best waterproof boots he could find. He noticed another man sitting near the river dressed in old, shabby clothes with a fishing rod next to him propped up against the rock he sat upon. The man on the rock looked friendly enough, but Soshi's captor decided he couldn't be bothered making small talk with someone so scruffily dressed. Besides, he still had some important things to do and didn't want to skin the animals with someone else so close by. He was on his way to make sure the kayakers were "fat and happy" as Grimes wanted them to be on their trip down the river. Even Juice had to admit the area was idyllic, with his own preference for congested cities. Natural environments frequently made him uncomfortable, like he was prey, being the hunted one. That was why he liked catching and skinning, for each animal he killed, it was one less that could harm him.

Juice stumbled a couple of times from the underbrush that seemed thicker and more dense as he approached the river. Good thing he purchased the most expensive boots the sporting goods store sold, he thought to himself. His feet were protected, he sprayed three cans of insect repellent all over his body, wore gloves, long sleeves and a hat with a patch of a large, growling grizzly bear on the front. He saw the kayakers slowly paddling toward him. He didn't see Grimes yet among the group. So he leaned against a tree and waited.

Chapter 26
Doc Ray

Abbie watched Mr. Toad's little tongue snap out and grab the insects he uncovered near some rotting wood. She never could watch him eat, it was so un-doglike. Her most preferred way of eating was to be fed with chopsticks by her mom. Her stomach had started to growl from hunger by now, but she knew she would wait for the pizza scraps Myrtle said she would bring for dinner tonight. Mr. Toad finally felt like he had finished his breakfast and said, "Well, are you ready?" "I've been ready. I've been lying here watching you eat. I will never be a fussy eater again when we get home," she said. "Let's go then," he said. "To where? Where should we go, what are we looking for?" Abbie asked him. Abbie was going to leave Myrtle a note, saying they would be back before dark, but then remembered Myrtle didn't know how to read. So she had to awaken her to tell her. "Will you both just go so I can get some sleep?" Myrtle asked irritably.

The two of them left the shed and decided to look for Gabe. She walked carefully with Mr. Toad on her back. They retraced their steps where they first met Myrtle the day before. They passed the area where Soshi's tunnel ended near the river's edge. There was no sign of Soshi, so they assumed he had returned back to the warren, going up the tunnel. They walked along slowly sniffing the area for familiar scents, when Abbie looked up at a shabbily dressed man sitting on a rock. He seemed to be expecting them and waved to them. "That is the same man in my dream I told you about," Abbie said to Mr. Toad. "Are you sure? The last thing we need is for someone to capture us," he answered. "It's all right, it's him, I tell you. Look, the sunshine is on just him, nothing else!" She ran over to him, glad to see a friendly face. She noticed even though he looked human, he had no human scent or any scent at all! How could that be? What she did notice was a feeling of kindness and peacefulness about him. She didn't notice what he was wearing only that she didn't feel hungry anymore. In fact, she felt quite healthy and strong. She looked into his eyes, which had a golden sparkle to them, similar to Gabe's.

"I've been waiting for you both, what took you so long?" the man said. "He had to have breakfast," Abbie said glancing over to Mr. Toad. "A growing man has to eat, what can I say?" Mr. Toad joked. "You can call me Doc Ray, that's what my friends call me," he replied. "Are you a veterinarian?" Abbie asked. "Well not exactly, but I'm pretty good at healing, no matter what or who needs to be healed," Doc Ray said. "Gabe and I frequently work together. We make a good team." "Can you help us? We weren't sure what we should do next," Mr. Toad said. "I'll take you right now where some help is needed. Let's go. I'll pick you both up onto my shoulder. Mr. Toad you can sit right next to Abbie, she's not that big after all." Doc Ray walked over to a large tree and stooped over to where there was a wire cage on the ground. He gently placed Abbie and Mr. Toad next to the cage. They looked in to find Soshi, the mink and raccoon pressed against the back of the cage as far away from the door as possible. Doc Ray lifted the latch, saying "Don't be afraid, I'm not the person who wants to harm you. I'm here to help you to safety. His soft voice had an immediate calming effect on them, so none of them tried to escape. The mink and raccoon slowly walked out, while Soshi remained in the cage, unable to walk. "Soshi!

What has happened to you?" Abbie shrieked. His vision was poor and he felt too weak to move. "I have just the thing he needs to feel better," Doc Ray said, reaching into the torn pocket of his shirt. It was only then that Abbie noticed how tattered his clothing was. He pulled out something that resembled soft taffy and told Soshi to swallow it. The rabbit was so weak, he couldn't resist or question what he was being given. He swallowed a very small piece of the sticky substance and laid back in the cage. "What happened to him?" Abbie asked Doc Ray. "He didn't know that the grass stalks he had eaten were toxic to him. He was poisoned by the very vegetation he has eaten all his life. He is only one of many who have been harmed by human actions against the Creator's plan," Doc Ray explained. "Then why were Soshi and the others locked in this cage?" Abbie asked. "That is the perverse hobby of someone who enjoys inflicting pain on little creatures," the Angel said. "Ohhhhhh!" the mink and raccoon both exclaimed together.

Soshi looked up at the voices around him and noticed he could see clearly and his headache was gone. He could feel his strength coming back, so he jumped up on his hind legs after recognizing Mr. Toad and Abbie a few feet away. "Wow! That was a fast recovery!" Mr. Toad excitedly exclaimed. He had thought for sure Soshi would not have survived much longer in the cage. "What's in that taffy anyway?" Abbie asked Doc Ray. "It's a special formula, can't really say what's in it, but it works all the time if someone has faith that it will help them," he said. "I think we need to leave this area now before the owner of this cage returns. I'll help all of you along and then I'll be on my way," Doc Ray said. He picked up the cage and they all followed him as it seemed the natural thing to do, heading toward the shed.

"Whoa! Stop! What do you think you are doing stealing my cage and the pelts in it?" Juice roared at Doc Ray. The little group was stunned to see a man thundering toward them and Doc Ray. They saw his huge frame clumsily running and jumping over roots and rocks with a snarling expression on his face. None of the animals had ever seen a human so angry before. Doc Ray had stopped guiding them and stood there looking at the angry large man moving closer and closer to them. The man screamed at Doc Ray saying, "Put that cage down!" Doc Ray gently placed the empty cage on the ground. The animals cowered behind him for protection. "Who do you think you are, you bum? I don't have to put up with people like you, in fact the world doesn't need people like you. You need to be taught a lesson for stealing other people's property." With one quick move, he grabbed the large knife from its sheath and lunged forward to Doc Ray, intending to strike him on the neck. Doc Ray did not move or try to protect himself, he just stood there. Abbie could not believe this was happening. "Why doesn't he do something?" she asked herself. Suddenly the large man lost his balance, as he was standing on uneven ground and started to fall backward. The full force the man had put into his intended attack on Doc Ray caused the sharp blade of the knife to pierce and slash his own thigh instead. He screamed in pain as blood gushed out of his self-inflicted wound. Doc Ray kindly asked the injured man if he needed some help, but the man loudly refused, shrieking more offensive sounds and words that did not seem to be very friendly. They heard him wailing on the ground as they walked away from the river toward the shed, wondering if they would ever see him again.

Chapter 27

Curious Thumbs

oc Ray led the little group back to the shed where they could sit in safety and decide what to do next. He smiled at them and gave Abbie a little kiss on her head, saying she was the cutest little Shih Tzu he had ever seen. She instinctively gave him some wet kisses on his cheek and noticed not only did he not have any human scent but his skin felt infinitely smooth with a fresh taste that she had never before experienced. How could someone with such shabby clothes be so different from the many humans she had met before, she thought. She realized that since she had met him that day, she wasn't hungry or thirsty either, but had a pleasant, contented feeling within her despite their frightful experiences. They watched him walk away with his fishing rod, until the leaves and shrubs interrupted their view of him. "Well, let's go inside where no one will see us. I don't know about you, but I don't want that guy with the knife finding us again," Mr. Toad said. Soshi was feeling back to normal and agreed. "Neither do I. He was going to skin us alive," he said speaking to the mink and young raccoon. "Something tells me he isn't going to be hunting any animals for awhile," Abbie said. "It seemed like a lot of blood coming out of his leg. I don't know why he didn't let Doc Ray help him." "I'm glad he didn't, that way he won't find us or other animals to skin," the mink said. "By the way, my name is Selena. I was just passing through, I normally don't live around here. It was time for me and my brothers and sisters to leave the litter so I was trying to find a nice safe place to make my home. I guess this is not the place," she said. "Oh but it usually is," Soshi said. "I have lived around here all my life, nothing like this has ever happened before. Don't leave now, you can stay with me at my place until things are safe again."

As they softly spoke, the young raccoon had started to explore the shed when something larger and heavier than he pounced on top of him. He gave out a loud cry and turned to see another raccoon on his back. "Dustin! What are you doing here?" Myrtle shrieked. "You shouldn't be away from the nest yet. My sister must be looking for you. Why are you away from home during the day?" "I was just curious, and wasn't sleepy when everyone else was during the day. I just wanted to walk around a little bit by myself, that's all," the adolescent raccoon said to his aunt. "And who are you two?" Myrtle asked Soshi and Selena. "What has happened while I slept that three more creatures are in this shed?" Abbie explained the happenings of the day and how Doc Ray had released Soshi, Selena and Dustin from the cage, healed Soshi and how the big man became angry and ended up injuring himself. "You need to stay here for now, and I will bring you back to your mother, before she goes out for food tonight, young man", Myrtle said. "Now I'm going back to sleep for a little while longer. I'd appreciate it if you all just kept your voices down to a dull roar," she said disgustedly, and climbed back up to the rafters of the shed and went back to sleep. None of them had ever seen a raccoon so upset before, but they knew she was only angry at what could have happened to Dustin because he was not experienced enough to be on his own yet.

Dustin was naturally curious and a little hyperactive. He found it very difficult to sit still and had to keep moving unless he became fascinated with something he had never seen before. While the others talked, he explored the walls and flooring of the shed. It didn't look anything like the hollowed out tree he and his family lived in. Soshi was trying to figure out how the group could get back up the tunnel to his warren up near the building. "I don't think that's such a good idea. We could bump into that guy with the knife. We don't know where he is. He could be right near the tunnel opening for all we know," Abbie said. She couldn't stop thinking about Doc Ray and how wonderful he was. "I agree", Mr. Toad said. "We were lucky to have escaped the knife guy, we probably wouldn't be so lucky again."

They heard a screechy sound at the rear of the shed and found Dustin pulling a board out of the wall, revealing a large opening that seemed to lead up a hill. Mr. Toad wondered if Dustin was like his Aunt Myrtle, who would now be bragging about how handy it was to have thumbs that could open just about anything. But Dustin didn't, he just said, "Hey, guys, look what I found." Soshi looked up the opening and thought it looked like it went straight up the hill toward the big red building and might be a good way to get back home. Abbie and Mr. Toad weren't sure if they should stay around the shed and river area or go back up the hill. Abbie really didn't like the idea of entering another dark hole, with no idea where it went, but remembered Gabe's words about not being afraid. Selena decided she would take Soshi's offer to stay with him for awhile. So they eventually decided they would follow Dustin up the clean, slippery slope in the hopes of finding safety and a new direction for their mission.

It was a surprisingly easy walk that appeared to be a tunnel of some sort. The walls were very smooth and clean. The only things in the tunnel were some thick cables attached to its floor, providing traction for them to walk on. Abbie really appreciated this as the pads on a dog's foot are very smooth. She wouldn't have been able to walk up such a steep incline and would have slid back down without the cables being there. They reached the top in a few minutes, where the tunnel ended near some structure with lots of other cables and wires going into it. They could hear and feel some something unusual coming out of the structure and decided it would be best it they avoided it. Dustin said his mother had told him and his litter mates whenever they came near something with wires that made strange humming sounds and made the fur stand up on their backs they should always stay away. They looked up and saw the big red brick building across the road. Mr. Toad had a brief flashback of his last encounter crossing this road but shook the memory out of his mind for the moment. "Let's go!" Abbie said. Mr. Toad jumped on her back and the five of them quickly crossed the road and ran up to the building. Soshi led the way as he knew exactly where he was. They followed him to the opening of his warren.

Chapter 28
Homeless

"We're almost there!" Soshi exclaimed to the little group, "We just have to get through all this mud...wait...what... why is it so wet here?" Soshi took another hop over to where the opening of his warren had been when the ground caved in, sending a large surface area of earth into the hole. "Oh Noooooo!" Soshi moaned, envisioning Julian being buried inside the warren with water and earth. "What has happened? We need to get Julian out of there" he pleaded to the others. Dustin was the first to come forward, saying, "It looks like there is a stream of water flowing into the hole." "It's not a hole! It's my home!" Soshi screamed. "I'm sorry, yes it's your home, but I don't think there's much left down there, it looks like it's full of water. This little stream of water has to be stopped first before anything can be done. There are some rocks and twigs over there, I can block the stream with them and redirect the flow of water. My mom and I watched how some beavers did that once; it took them awhile because they don't have thumbs like us raccoons do." Mr. Toad leaned to Abbie, whispering in her ear, saying, "I just knew he'd eventually start bragging about being a raccoon and having thumbs, it must run in the family." "Shhh," she said, "he is the only one who has thumbs. That does give him an advantage you know."

Dustin began redirecting the stream away from its course down the warren while Soshi stood and sobbed, his long floppy ears dripping with muddy water. He had stuck his head down the hole to see how much damage the flood had caused, only to extract himself with his face, whiskers and ears covered in mud. "I'm going to find out where the stream is coming from," Dustin announced. Anyone want to come with me?" "I will," Selena said. She had become enamored of Dustin's ingenuity and felt a bond with him from their shared frightful ordeal. They started to follow the source of the stream with the others trudging behind them. Soshi was last, walking the slowest, wondering if he had dreamt the events of the past day. How could so much have happened to him in twenty-four hours, he asked himself. Where was

Julian, were they homeless, would the man with the knife find him again? It was getting to be too much to think about. He found himself shaking with fear and sadness. Mr. Toad had hitched a ride on Abbie's back, something that had become the natural thing to do. He sat perched behind her neck holding onto the hair that had been in pigtails but now would fall over her eyes. It was an amusing sight to see a toad standing on her back at the base of her neck holding onto the hair of her head with his webbed hands like reins on a horse. It had become a mutually beneficial means of transportation for each of them. Besides not weighing very much, she liked having him so close to her; he was safe and they could talk to one another more easily.

They soon found the source of the water. It appeared to be spraying out of the ground from various places. All of a sudden, the water stopped, at all of the places, at once! "Well, I've never seen that before," Dustin declared. "I have," said Abbie. "There are certain places where the water sprays out over the same areas each day. I've seen that looking out of my windows up there," she said, lifting her face up toward the red brick building's glass panes high above them. They all just stood there wondering what to do next. Mr. Toad had the highest vantage point looking out over Abbie's round head. "Look! There is Slade," he said. "Let's go, walk straight ahead," he told Abbie. She did as he said, and started to catch Slade's scent before she was able to see him. "Slade! It's me, Mr. Toad!" he called out to the muskrat. "Well, so it is. Are you all right? It's been a hectic day. Are these all your friends?" he asked. Behind Abbie, stood Dustin, Selena and Soshi. "Yes, we were actually looking for you, Violet, the babies and Opal. Are they with you?" Mr. Toad asked. "Yes, yes, they are. We have a house guest too, a rabbit named Julian. Come, sit with us for awhile. They will be glad to see you again. We were worried about you." Soshi's ears stood straight up when he heard Julian's name. "Did you say there is a rabbit named Julian with you?" Soshi asked. "Why yes, his warren was flooded out so I invited him to stay with us for awhile," Slade replied. They followed the muskrat through the thickets and bushes down into a warm, dry area against the foundation of the building, to find a comfortable but crowded area filled with freshly harvested vegetation, baby muskrats, Violet, Opal and Julian.

Chapter 29
Lame Excuse

Juice looked at his watch. He had taken his shirt off to make a bandage for his thigh from both sleeves. The cut was very deep into the muscles, so blood still seeped through the fabric. He really didn't know what to do first. He had no first aid kit. He knew he probably needed to get to a hospital. He realized his body was now potentially exposed to bites from mutated insects and animals. In fact his leg was sticky from seeping blood, attracting some flies and other stinging insects. His frustrations with the buzzing insects led him to rinse his hands and his bandaged thigh with water from the river. He remembered what Grimes had said about not drinking the river water, and told himself as long as he didn't drink it, he would be fine. Besides, he knew where the tainted water was he thought, he had discharged the chemicals himself into a different part of the river. He had spent too much time tending to his wound, and was worried he may have missed his scheduled encounter with the kayakers and Grimes. Why hadn't Grimes called him back yet?

He had no sooner finished the thought when his phone vibrated through his pants pocket, causing his injury to sting even more. He carefully reached for the phone, trying to avoid any tension or stretching to his injured leg. His hands were sticky again after touching the bandage oozing blood from his thigh. He answered the call. "Hey there, Dude, where are you? My friends want to meet you," Grimes spoke with his smiling voice over the phone. He never spoke that way to Juice when they were alone. This meant Grimes was with people he wanted to impress, it must be his environmentalist friends Juice thought. He knew he was in no condition to walk down to the river, let alone meet Grimes' important associates. He had to think of some excuse to avoid the "meet and greet" Grimes had planned for him. Juice was supposed to be a friend of Grimes with shared environmental interests, who was familiar with the area and its native habitat. He would be someone who could describe the changes he had seen in the river environment, someone who had some credibility based on his healthy appearance, flashing smile and Grimes' fabricated descriptions of his intelligence, honesty and passion for the environment. When Grimes first told him about the role he would be portraying at the "meet and greet", Juice felt uncomfortable, and even said the character he would be playing was nothing like himself. But over time, the more he thought about the character he would be playing, the more he believed he could become that character. However, his present condition did not make him feel like the persona Grimes had created. It was then that Juice realized what Grimes' plan was all about. He wanted to create a world where everyone and everything would not exist in its natural state, but would live and behave in ways he wanted people and lifeforms to be. A world in which he would have tremendous power over what kind of communication people would receive, creating worry and panic.

Juice decided to tell Grimes he was delayed because he had been in a motor vehicle accident and would have to meet his friends at a later date. Grimes would know this was an excuse, as

Juice had an apartment within walking distance and did not need a vehicle to get to the river. Juice knew Grimes would be furious, yet wouldn't let his group know that he was angry. Instead he would probably tell them he hoped no one was injured in the mishap. Grimes could tell that something had happened to Juice when he made the phone call by his voice, which was soft and shaky. Grimes asked, "So are you all right? You don't sound very good, my friend. Do you need 911?" "No, I'm all right, just can't get there right now," Juice answered. He pressed the red "end" button on his phone to disconnect the call. His thigh had begun to seep more blood through the makeshift bandage. He didn't have anything else to wrap his leg with and had started to feel light-headed. He hadn't taken any bottled water with him and was feeling very thirsty. He lost consciousness after hitting his head on a large rock as he fell to the ground.

Chapter 30
A Furry Council

It was quite crowded in the warren, with Slade, Violet, the baby muskrats, Opal, Dustin, Selena, Abbie, Mr. Toad, Soshi and Julian in it. But despite the closeness of their furry bodies, there was an air of excitement and happiness. Opal had brought in some various greens and rhizomes, Mr. Toad had slurped some tasty insects along the route to the warren, and Selena and Dustin had found some birds' eggs that had fallen out of a nest. Abbie noticed she still was not hungry after giving Doc Ray some wet kisses on his face and was grateful for this. There was nothing in the warren that appealed to her for dinner. The little group shared stories about what they had either seen themselves or learned from talking to other animals along the river. Abbie and Mr. Toad spoke about Gabe and Doc Ray. Soshi told how he had almost died after eating the tainted shoots at the river, except for Doc Ray giving him something that tasted like peanut butter. Dustin and Selena described how they were captured by the big man who had plans to skin them alive with his big knife for their pelts. "Me too!" interjected Soshi. "He was planning to do that to me as well, until Doc Ray came along with Abbie and Mr. Toad. I wonder how he knew just where to find us," he reflected.

Just then, there was a large thud at the opening of the warren, accompanied by a very loud, "HA! I found you. What on earth on you doing here?" Myrtle roared at Dustin. "It's a good thing my senses are so keen to have found you. Although I must say it was easier having that dog scent to help locate you." Myrtle dropped a large square box from her hands to the ground in the middle of the group. The others did not move, staring at the raccoon, wondering why she was there. "I told you I'd take you back to your mother, but I also told the dog I'd get her a pizza for dinner. I always keep my word, as all raccoons do, we are very reliable with excellent memories." At this, Mr. Toad hopped onto Abbie's shoulders again, saying softly in her ear, "If she starts about the virtues of raccoons again..." he said. "Shhh! That's just the way they are. You have to admit, she has some advantages the rest of us don't have that are helpful," Abbie said to him carefully.

Twelve pairs of eyes turned to the square box. Abbie read the words which said in large letters PIZZA, printed all over it. She had seen boxes like these before when her mom had them delivered to the apartment. She knew she liked pizza, especially the kind with cheese and meatballs on it. This one actually smelled good. Myrtle opened the box and the others peered into it, smelling the new aromas. Abbie looked at the lid again and noticed it was labeled "The Works", meaning that just about everything you could put on a pizza was on it, so there was literally something for everyone there to eat. It truly was a little feast to celebrate their gathering.

Every crumb, crust and particle of topping was soon finished by the group. Mr. Toad had hopped into the box, so his long tongue could scour the bottom for any traces left that the others might have missed. Myrtle announced, "OK, OK, it's night time and that means my day is just beginning. Dustin, tell me how you came to be friends with this furry group before I take you back home." Mr. Toad glared at her and really wanted to remind her he did not have any fur or much in common with the rest of the animals. The parotid glands on his back had begun to itch, the way they did when he became agitated. Feeling somewhat detached from all the mammals, it took all his energy to stay seated next to Abbie and not jump into Myrtle's face just to show her how agile toads could be. Abbie sensed his frustration as she watched his bulging eyes dart back and forth as Myrtle spoke. She glanced at him, whispering "No!" under her breath. He glared back at her, but knew she was right. Sometimes he felt lonely being the only amphibian among the group. He had no family, never knew what a mother and father were until he met the muskrats. It seemed like mammals were so different from him. They could somehow relate to one another. He wondered if humans were mammals too; they didn't have fur covering their bodies, but they seemed like they could get along with one another. He had seen lots of humans walking and talking with one another when he and Abbie would spend hours looking out the sunny windows of their apartment. But the man with the knife was different. He had never met a human so angry and dangerous before. He recognized the anger within himself could become like the anger the man with the knife had, and was glad Abbie was there with him to help him calm down.

Dustin began to tell his aunt the events of the past two days. Soshi explained how he was poisoned by the river grass and would have died without Doc Ray's help. Julian described how his warren became flooded, leading him to stay with the muskrat family. Myrtle listened carefully, visualizing each detail in her mind. She was familiar with the area and had never seen the big man with the knife or the shabbily dressed man called Doc Ray, but had noticed changes in some of the wildlife near the river. Abbie and Mr. Toad told everyone Gabe's explanation about the cause of the changes at the river. Myrtle decided she needed to speak with the older raccoons and beavers who had lived in the area longer than she had, to get their advice. Everyone was excited and talking at once, making such a cacophony it sounded like a small zoo. Abbie was getting a headache from the noise and Mr. Toad's parotid glands started to hum again. "OK, let's calm down and decide what we're going to do," Abbie said.

Chapter 31
Without A Leg To Stand On

It was late afternoon when Juice regained consciousness. He was too weak to walk, and had started to painstakingly pull himself along on the ground. The phone in his pocket buzzed again. He reached down and answered the call, seeing it was Grimes. He really didn't want to speak with him, but knew he was the only person who could help him. "Yeah, what are you doing? What happened to you? I hope my friends believed the story about your car accident. If this thing fails because of your stupidity, you will be the sorriest person on earth, I promise you that," Grimes yelled into the phone. "I need help. I fell and my leg is badly hurt. I can't walk," Juice said softly. He didn't have much strength left and was trying to not lose consciousness again before the phone call ended. "Just where are you?" Grimes demanded. He knew he couldn't leave Juice on the ground and risk someone finding him. Who could know what Juice would say about why he was lying on the ground injured. "Give me some landmarks I can use to find you. Are you near the road? How far away from the river are you?" "I don't know exactly where I am, probably closer to the river than the road. I can hear the power plant's turbines where I am. There's a lot of underbrush and dried mud and dead branches where I am. That's how I tripped and fell," Juice explained.

Juice didn't tell Grimes that he lost his balance trying to attack Doc Ray, he knew that would just infuriate Grimes even more right now. "All right, I've got a little time right now to come out and find you. Keep your phone next to you. I'll call you again after I get closer to you." Grimes was annoyed with Juice that he had to use up some time he had planned to spend with his environmentalist friends. It was getting late in the day now and he had to change his plans with them to find Juice. They were disappointed at not being able to meet Juice, after Grimes' description of his impressive strength and great knowledge of the river's environment.

Grimes arrived at the wooded area near the river, driving along the road until he could hear the power plant's turbines. He decided not to park too close to the power plant after noticing its parking area was full of vehicles. He took his binoculars out of the storage area of his luxury SUV to read the names of the official government agencies lettered on the vehicles' doors. Uttering some obscenities under his breath and wondering why they were there, he decided to move his own vehicle further away from the power plant. He entered the wooded area again selecting Juice's phone number from his phone contact list.

Chapter 32
Six Too Many

"So this is where the gloves were found in the storage area? And gloves like these are never used by anyone who works here? Is it possible that someone brought his own gloves in to work instead of using the ones provided by the plant?" The State Police detectives had been called by the power plant manager after employees found a different type of protective glove in the chemical storage area and notified the manager. Since the hydroelectric generation plant was on the river, complying with numerous environmental and anti-pollution laws was always a priority. Any possibility of unauthorized entry to the facility was taken very seriously. "We've had the same employees working here for over ten years. They are well trained, valuable employees who wouldn't take a chance not using the safety equipment we provide for them. In fact, they only need gloves to handle the lubricants for the generators and some cleaning solvents. Nothing really hazardous. We don't need many people here, the generators operate 24 hours a day. In fact we only have one twelve hour shift seven days a week," the plant manager explained. "That's why I became suspicious when we found those gloves. They are the type that are used more for exposure to chemicals in a laboratory than an industrial setting like ours."

The detectives took photos of the interior of the plant, the area where the gloves were found and then more photos of the exterior of the building. They returned inside to speak with the plant manager again. "Anything else touched or missing?" they asked. "Nothing is missing that's for sure. We took an inventory of everything. The only thing we noticed was there were a few more containers of lubrication chemicals than our inventory system said we had. Nothing else unusual", the manager explained. "What do you mean, your inventory of lubrication liquids was more than you thought?" one of the older detectives asked. "Everything that comes in and goes out of this building is entered in our digital inventory. That way we know when to order more supplies," the manager said. "Can you show us where those containers are?" the detective asked. They walked over to the storage area with the manager, who pointed to the containers saying, "Here they are, there are six more containers here than our inventory system said that we had. This is where the different pair of gloves was found as well."

The detectives examined the containers, noticing that six of them were almost empty. They opened the lid and looked inside, then showed them to the manager. "That's strange," the manger said, our lubricants are quite thick and a grayish-green in color. The liquid of these containers is clear and more aqueous." "We're going to take these six containers back with us and have them analyzed, something is not right here. Do you have a surveillance system here?" the younger detective asked. "We do, but it doesn't cover the exterior of the building, just some interior areas near the generators and this storage area. We would have to review the past thirty days though, since we don't know when this unauthorized entry occurred," the manager explained. "We would like to have the disk, we'll have someone look at it for you," the detective said. The manager and detectives went back to the office and removed the closed circuit camera recording. "We'll let you know what we find and get back to you. Anything else suspicious, please let us know right away." The detectives drove away with the hunch that something treacherous was happening in the area.

Chapter 33
Betrayal

Juice answered his phone after several rings. He found he could not move very quickly, even to only pick up the phone. His fingers felt bigger and clumsy. He heard Grimes' annoyed voice say, "OK, do you have Location Services turned on? I can find you that way faster than you trying to tell me where you are." Juice was relieved to hear this, as he had no idea exactly where he was, saying, "Yeah, I do." Grimes found Juice propped against one of the fallen trees on the mossy ground. He knew at once Juice had lost a lot of blood and was in and out of consciousness. "How did this happen? Who did this to you?" Grimes asked, wondering how he was going to get Juice out of the area and back to his apartment. "It was… an…. accident. J-J-J-Just get me out of here please," Juice pleaded. Grimes pulled him up and grabbed the arm on the uninjured side of his body, and told him to lean on him so they could walk out to his vehicle. It took awhile, as Juice wasn't able to bear his own weight very well and kept stumbling over his own feet. They finally reached Grimes' SUV. He had to push Juice's body into the back seat, as Juice was too weak to get in by himself.

Grimes drove the short distance to Juice's apartment. He didn't want anyone to notice Juice's bloodstained pants, so he wrapped a blanket around him to make it appear as though Juice was only intoxicated, and he was just taking a good friend home after a day of drinking. He brought him upstairs to his apartment and laid him on a couch near a window overlooking the street. "You're not going to leave me alone are you?" Juice pitifully asked him. "I need to see a doctor for my leg." "I'll be back to take you to a hospital, don't worry. I just have to run an errand first, my friends are waiting for me. I'll drive by and blow the horn, you can wave hello to them. They're disappointed they couldn't meet you." Grimes lied. He had no intention of returning to the apartment. He removed the battery to Juice's phone without his knowledge and handed it back to him. "I'll see you later," he grinned as he walked out the door.

Grimes was initially angry with Juice for not meeting him with his kayaker friends, but he now realized this turn of events solved a gnawing problem he had: what to do with Juice after the project was over. All he had to do was leave him alone in his apartment, without a phone and unable to get help. He would be dead within twelve hours. His plan to gain wealth, fame and revenge would be safe.

Chapter 34
The Beavers

Myrtle, Abbie and Mr. Toad left the group to meet with the beavers Myrtle said she knew. "Follow me. I'll take you there," she said. Mr. Toad hopped onto Abbie shoulders again, holding onto the hair of her head and her ears. This had become his preferred mode of traveling since it afforded them both speed and the opportunity to talk while walking. Since beavers and raccoons are both members of the rodent family, it didn't seem too unrealistic to them that she knew the beavers in the area. Abbie and Mr. Toad had never met a beaver before and really didn't know what to expect. They trusted Myrtle that she wouldn't bring them to any harm, but there was always some doubt in Mr. Toad's mind. They had to cross the road, walk down the grassy hill and into the un-landscaped hillside toward the river.

It was starting to get dark by now and the three of them had varying degrees of nocturnal vision, with Abbie being the least nocturnal. She looked up at the sky and thought for a moment she could see some stars sparkling in the early dusk, making her think of Gabe. She wondered if he was watching and knew where they were going. Myrtle pushed through the underbrush easily with her powerful arms. Abbie moved more slowly without the advantage of opposing thumbs and not wanting to have Mr. Toad knocked off her shoulders. They walked past the area where Soshi, Dustin and Selena had been trapped and thought they could hear coyotes howling, but decided it would be best if they stayed focused on their mission to find the beavers. Myrtle suddenly stopped short, causing Abbie's flat face to almost meet Myrtle's long fluffy tail. Before anyone could speak, Gabe appeared to them on the path saying, "Mr. Toad, come with me, there is someone you need to have a 'man-to-man' conversation with." The raccoon was speechless for once, having just met Gabe face to face. "Oh Gabe, I was just thinking about you, wondering if we would see you again," Abbie said. She was hoping he would pick her up and give her a hug, feeling like she needed someone to love her at that moment. Knowing her thoughts, he bent down and gently placed her on his shoulder, letting her give him some soft licks on his neck.

Myrtle continued to stare up at him, still at a loss for words, realizing that Gabe was not like anyone she had ever met before. He said, "Abbie and Myrtle, you can continue on to meet with the beavers." He put Abbie back down tenderly, making eye contact that let her know she could trust him with her life. Gabe seemed to disappear with Mr. Toad as quickly as he had appeared a moment earlier.

After slogging through watery mud and tree branches piled on top of one another, they suddenly heard the sharp sound of something slapping the surface of the water. Abbie was startled and correctly interpreted the sound as some kind of warning. "You stay here," Myrtle snapped at her. "The beavers have probably caught the scent of a dog and are telling you to not come any closer." They know me but I will have to meet with them alone first, and tell them it is safe for you to enter their territory. Beavers are one of the only animals who have a keener sense of smell than raccoons, but we have thumbs." Abbie thought Mr. Toad would probably tell Myrtle off one day about the merits of toads, but knew this was not the place nor time to do so. Abbie was grateful to have a few moments of rest after such a rigorous walk.

Myrtle moved cautiously over the felled trees covering the deep water. Even if she fell through she was a strong swimmer, but she knew that anyone from the beaver family could suddenly pop out of the water, ready to defend its territory. The beavers were much larger and stronger, so she respected their capabilities. Suddenly, she found herself staring into the long face of a large male beaver, who had pushed himself through the branches in the water and into her path.

"I've been following you for awhile before I recognized your scent, Myrtle," Varun said. "Oh my!" Myrtle exclaimed, surprised that she didn't detect his scent so near to her. It must have been that most of his body was still underwater. "I need to speak with you about something. But first, you need to know I am with a friend of mine: a dog." "I know about the dog, my sons picked up the canine scent as soon as it entered our territory. They won't let them pass, you know that. Beavers don't trust dogs. They are frequently accompanied by those humans who always want to trap and kill us," Varun said with anger in his voice. "Yes, I know what you mean, and that is usually the case. But this is different, I promise you. This is a small dog, unaccompanied by a human, who has a toad for a friend," Myrtle explained.

"A small dog you say? Without a human?" Myrtle said, "I know, it's not what you'd expect, but that is just my point. Please let her enter your dam." Varun was deciding whether or not to trust Myrtle, staring at her with his small, beady eyes. Beavers do not have good vision, so he had to rely on his excellent olfactory senses to determine if Myrtle or the dog were stressed or angry. He made some barking and grunting sounds toward his sons and within a minute they surfaced next to him. "The dog is all right. We'll let this one in, but only this one. No other dogs," Varun told them. "OK, tell your dog friend to enter the dam and we can all talk." Myrtle stepped back over the branches of the dam to where Abbie was waiting. "It's OK. Varun said you can enter. This is the first time a dog has ever been given permission to enter the dam area," Myrtle explained. "Beavers usually only associate with their own kind you know. They rarely even bother with raccoons."

They slowly walked on the surface of the dam, which was really multiple layers of fallen trees and branches. It didn't look very organized, but in reality was carefully engineered by the beaver family to protect them from predators by creating a beaver pond around their lodge. Abbie and Myrtle walked to the end of the dam and waited for their host to greet them. As they were staring at the water beyond the dam, Varun pulled himself up on the dam behind them. Abbie was the first to notice a pungent smell in the air, and was just about to comment on it when Myrtle turned and said, "Ah, there you are. This is the friend I told you about. You can see, she is quite harmless to you, who easily outweigh her four times over." "I'm Varun, what is your name? And why are you here?" "I'm Abbie," she said to the very large beaver. Abbie told him how the saga began after meeting with Gabe and hearing about the environmental damage caused by a corrupt man wanting to create his own lifeforms.

Varun listened carefully, recalling some of the genetic atrocities he had seen on the river, and sadly within his own family. "I know what you mean. Our last litter of kits was born with some problems I have never seen before with baby beavers. All three of them have tiny tails, hardly any fur and no teeth! They don't swim very well either. How will they be able survive on their own? My wife and I are heartbroken. None of our other children have ever looked like that. We know that another beaver family had some kits with some problems, and they all died before they were a year old. My wife and I and our older children are doing everything we can to help them grow, but nothing we do seems to benefit them. I don't even think they have any vision at all." Varun turned his head away as tears started to fall from his small brown eyes. Abbie couldn't help but notice some similarities between Varun and Slade, although Slade was much smaller in size and didn't have as strong an odor. Varun said, "I will help you in any way I can to stop this horror. Even though beavers usually keep within our own families, when there is a common threat to our lives and territory, we can work together very effectively."

Just then, the beating of wings swooped over their heads. They all looked up together, but only Abbie recognized the danger they were in with nowhere to go for protection. As the big owl hovered over them, she thought it was the last moment of her life, expecting to be grabbed and eaten by the hungry bird. Instead, the owl landed right next to them, saying, "I just heard what you said. I saw how this happened. I saw a man pouring some liquid into the water near the power plant at night. Not long after that, life on the river changed. My own eggs could not hatch because the shells were too soft and broke while in my nest. My baby birds never had a chance to hatch." "Beryl, when did this happen?" Varun asked the owl. "A few weeks ago. How are your kits, are they growing? I haven't seen them yet," she asked. Varun answered her, "Not doing well. My wife is very worried. They aren't growing, they can't swim well yet, they're still in the lodge, and if they can't swim, how can they leave the lodge? Can you show me where that man poured the liquid in the water?" Varun asked Beryl. "I can organize all the beavers and within a day or so, we can block the flow of water in that area to isolate that stuff. It will just settle to the bottom of the river and not spread to do anymore harm." "Myrtle asked, "Do you really think other beaver families will work with your family?" "After I explain the problems with my young kits, they would be willing to help, I just know it. We love our families and always want to protect them," Varun explained.

They all agreed this would be the best plan and Varun would begin to contact the other beaver families that night and start making a new dam immediately. Myrtle and Abbie stepped back over the tree limbs and branches back on solid ground, being very careful not to swallow any of the water that splashed onto their faces. It was the first time Abbie realized how quickly this evil plan could destroy the lives of innocent animals, including themselves. Varun and the other beavers would be working in the most toxic part of the contaminated water to save the food chain for their families and countless others.

Chapter 35
Caught On Camera

"Hey look at this!" the younger detective called to his partner investigating the apparent break-in at the power plant. "I'll be right there. I'm just printing out the analytical chemical report of the stuff in those six extra containers. It's not any kind of industrial lubricant, the lab says it some kind of highly concentrated solvent used in gene splicing or genetic experiments. It's nothing that any chemical supply company would even sell, never mind stock. It's highly toxic to anything with DNA, so that's all plants and animals! What do you have?" The younger detective had found the segment on the surveillance disk showing a tall, well built man entering the plant's storage area carrying two of the containers and placing them on the floor near the other similar-looking containers. A few minutes later, he was carrying in two more of the containers. Several minutes later, he returned with the last two containers. He took what appeared to be a flashlight and scanned the containers with it. The detective thought it strange, as he couldn't see any light coming out of the flashlight. The older detective exclaimed, "Wow! That's pretty slick, he has an ultra-violet flashlight to identify something on the containers. We need to examine those containers with UV light."

Chapter 36

Angry & Confused

Juice lay on his couch unable to move. The throbbing in his leg had spread so that his whole body ached; he felt hot and very thirsty, but not hungry. It seemed like Grimes had been gone a very long time. He fumbled for his phone, having the thought he should call 911. He tried to turn it on several times, but nothing happened. He looked out the window and noticed the shabbily dressed man he had seen in the woods, standing across the street looking at him. Why was this bum there, it was supposed to be Grimes, where was he? He screamed at Doc Ray, picked up his phone and threw it through the window toward him. The phone crashed through the glass and landed on the sidewalk. Doc Ray waved and disappeared. Juice became scared, and thought maybe he should have asked the man for help.

The effort it took for Juice to throw the phone through the window left him more exhausted. It seemed like he was going to black out again. He closed his eyes and then opened them after hearing a voice say, "Did you say 'man-to-man' talk?" Mr. Toad was asking Gabe what he meant by this, but was astounded to have found himself instantly face to face with the big man who had trapped Soshi, Dustin and Selena. He turned his head and found Gabe sitting on a chair out of the range of Juice's vision. It all seemed very strange, but Mr. Toad knew that anything seemed to be possible with Gabe.

Juice felt as though he had blacked out again, speaking to a toad in his apartment. Mr. Toad's anger overcame his fear of Juice and asked, "What makes you want to hurt helpless animals?" Juice mumbled, "I never thought about it. Maybe because someone told me my father left us to go to Canada to trap animals for furs. I barely remember him." "Well, at least you had a father," Mr. Toad responded angrily. Juice went on, "The first time I trapped, I wanted to see what it was like, to maybe get to know what he was like, what he thought about. I didn't really know who I was, had no goals in my life. It was awful at first, especially with the very young animals. Weird, but in a way, they reminded me of myself, helpless, begging for a chance to live. I didn't like feeling like that, so I made believe I was my father, the strong one, the guy in control. It didn't bother me anymore after that and helped me to get by. My mother who was a weak woman, had started to drink too much." Juice paused, and tears welled up in his eyes. "The State took me away from her, I got angry. I got moved from one foster home to another. I turned 18 and joined the military, but got kicked out for insubordination, I never liked following the rules. I remember being more angry because I felt so different from the people who knew their fathers, like I was the only one who didn't. I went from job to job, and then saw Professor Grimes' advertised position. It seemed like I could finally do something worthwhile, like 'work on a scientific experiment'. I guess he was a kind of father figure for me, he said he'd take me on as an apprentice." Juice's eyes were focused on Mr. Toad, who was standing on the knee of his uninjured leg, just in front of his face.

Mr. Toad realized he had something in common with this man whom he had feared: the anger at not having a family of his own. He asked himself how he could have the same feelings as this person who had wanted to kill his friends and other innocent animals just for a sense of power. He remembered what Gabe had said to him about how confusion and deceit have been in the world since the first humans chose to not obey the Creator's one rule. He stared at Juice and noticed he had stopped talking, his whole body had begun to shake, his eyes rolled up and then closed. Mr. Toad looked up at Gabe, who had been silent the whole time, and asked, "Is he dead?" "No, but it's time for us to leave. Someone is calling 911; they'll be on their way now to take him to a hospital. Let's go."

Chapter 37

Our Father

Mr. Toad was back on Gabe's shoulders in a quiet, dimly lit building, It was pleasantly peaceful in there with candles flickering in the soft light. "So what's so special about fathers that not having one can make me angry?" he asked Gabe. "All earthly creatures have a biological father and mother. Different creatures have varying degrees of involvement with their fathers. But earthly parents are not perfect creatures, and sometimes they make mistakes. That is why the only perfect parent is our Creator, the only true Father of everyone, for toads, animals, humans and angels. The Truth and Trust we all seek can only come from The Father, that's why there is never any confusion or deception from Him. He provides for all of our support, according to our needs," Gabe explained. "So I do have a Father after all who cares about me?" Mr. Toad asked feeling reassured. "You and all creatures do. It is His Love for all His creation. You see, this is the message you and Abbie were called upon to deliver. There are many diverse creatures on this earth. If you accept the Father's unconditional love for you in your heart, then it is easy to care for one another out of Love for one another."

Chapter 38

Maybe Not Hallucinating?

The county 911 operator had received a phone call with the caller ID reading "Unknown" for a medical emergency at Juice's address. She thought someone must have hacked into their phone system for a crank call, as all phone numbers going to 911 had to have an identifying phone number, name and address or some kind of relevant information. She thought about reporting this to her supervisor, but decided to play it safe in case the call was legitimate. She notified the local EMS personnel, who immediately went on the call to Juice's address. They entered his apartment, to find him semi-conscious and delirious on the couch, with shards of glass from the broken window scattered in the room. Taking him out of the building, one of the paramedics noticed the mobile phone on the ground in front of the shattered window that Juice had thrown at Doc Ray. He picked it up thinking that the phone could belong to this man, and would give it to the local police.

The hospital was a 15 minutes drive. Two EMT's were attending to Juice; one communicating his vital signs to the hospital emergency unit nurse and the other stabilizing his condition for the ride. The third EMT driving the van was trying to figure out how someone with such a large gash on his leg could have ended up on his own couch. No knife was near him and it didn't appear that his injury was inflicted in his apartment. He would just write his report and forward it to police detectives along with the mobile phone.

Juice was treated by emergency staff and later moved to an observation room due to his delirium, infection and likelihood for surgery. "I don't know what happened to this guy, but his stories are very interesting," one nurse told her shift replacement. "He's having a conversation with a toad or frog. It must be the fever and infection he has. Poor guy. Have fun with him."

The next morning, Juice's medical condition had worsened. Doctors were discussing the possibility that amputation of Juice's leg would be necessary due to loss of blood to the limb. He was still delirious, and talking about a toad who sat on his leg, genetic experiments and trapping animals to be like his father. The staff needed to know if he was psychotic and able to consent to surgery, and decided to have a psychologist evaluate his mental status. After spending an hour with Juice, the psychologist felt that although Juice's ramblings were indeed strange, there was consistency and his judgment and capacity for decision-making was intact. He was feeling a little stronger and could converse much better now than when he was admitted to the hospital.

Chapter 39
Toxin

The older detective had just checked his email after arriving at the State Police barracks office. There it was: the identification of the chemical found in the power plant containers. The chemical formula was listed as highly experimental, and belonged to a Professor Thomas Grimes, with an affiliation to a major West Coast university. A rating of its hazards, storage requirements and expiration dates from manufacture were listed as well. This formula became more hazardous when placed in ordinary sunlight, so that the longer the exposure, the more destructive it became to the nucleic acids, which are the building blocks of DNA. "Why would anyone want to deliberately make something like this?" he asked the younger detective. "How did this stuff end up here, on the East Coast?" he wondered aloud.

He decided they needed to find the whereabouts of this Professor Thomas Grimes as soon as possible. He checked the phone extension directory to call his supervisor's office for legal advice on how to proceed.

Chapter 40
Chaos on the River

Juice's injury had disrupted Grimes' plans for his environmentalist friends to observe and inquire about the changed lifeforms on the river. He had planned spending more time kayaking along the river's edge, talking with Juice, which would have provided adequate time for the group to notice the aberrations in waterfowl and insects. It had taken several months to organize this little group of powerful environmental activists whose opinions were frequently quoted in mainstream media. Not being able to meet Juice cut short their excursion and they insisted that Grimes check on Juice after his supposed motor vehicle accident instead of continuing their tour of the river. Grimes had to devise another way to get them back on the river, but would they really want to spend more hours kayaking in the same area again? He could appear very sincere and affable when situations necessitated changes in his demeanor. He decided he would ask them to help him locate a missing solar powered closed circuit camera that Juice was supposed to find that day but was now unable to work due to his "accident". Grimes presented a very convincing explanation to the group about the importance of the camera to his research, which was a complete fabrication. When the group immediately agreed to help with a search for the camera, Grimes couldn't contain his elation and amazement, that it was so easy to manipulate this group of prominent individuals.

They all agreed to meet right after breakfast the following morning, so that they would be ready to leave by mid-afternoon. Grimes had offered to drive them to the airport where their private jet would be waiting to take them home. Grimes briefly thought about Juice, assuming he would have died sometime during the previous night. He felt relieved about not having to see Juice again, but decided to drive by his apartment building anyway. He slowed down as he passed the property, noticing that the window of Juice's apartment was partially shattered. He didn't notice anything else unusual, but decided not to stay in the area very long, in case Juice was still alive in there.

Grimes had told his friends to leave their kayaks on the shore and that Juice would be moving them back to his home later, so when they arrived at the river, everything was just as they had left it the day before. They were excited about being part of Grimes' "experiment" and decided that in the best interest of time, they should start out in a different area from where they were yesterday. One of the women suggested they go further north, since they had already paddled by the area to the south of where they were. The other five immediately agreed with her before Grimes could propose going further south, where he felt there would be greater chances of coming in contact with affected animals and insects. There was no logical reason to dispute her rationale, so he decided to follow their lead, despite a growing sense of uneasiness at not being in total control of the outing. They paddled up the river for about fifteen minutes, before they heard the sound of saplings crashing down on the water. The lead kayaker stopped paddling and motioned to the others to do the same. They decided to get off the river and walk on land to see what was happening, and also they reasoned, maybe they could find the missing camera in the area. They soon came upon several beavers chopping down saplings and small trees so they would fall into the river. It looked like they were trying to stop the water's flow the way they were positioning the felled trees and brush. There were two more beavers swimming in the water pushing some tree trunks that had long since rotted off their stumps into the same area.

"Well, would you look at that!" a man wearing a white cap, with the earth embroidered in green and over the earth two gold-embroidered clasping hands said. "These beavers are in a hurry to build a dam during the daytime. They usually do this only at night. What could be making them do that at this hour?" The beavers had noticed the group, having smelled them as they disembarked from the kayaks, but decided to continue their work anyway. After learning about the toxin in the river, they figured humans were a lesser danger to their survival than usual. Before Grimes could redirect the group away from the beavers, the man with the white cap had started taking a video of the beavers. He noticed there was a lodge on the river about thirty feet in. He convinced the others to help him drag some dead tree limbs over to the lodge, to have something to which to tie their kayaks. Then they could paddle over to the lodge to get a better look at it. None of them had ever been this close to a beaver lodge before and the thought of taking some photos of beavers this close was intriguing to them. Grimes was not sure if this deviation was going to benefit his plan for the group, but felt he would let them explore the area anyway.

The water was only about seven feet deep around the beaver lodge. The four men and two women were physically fit and able to accomplish their goal within a half hour. They had almost finished lashing their kayaks to the branches around the lodge when suddenly two kayaks were toppled over, sending one of the women and a man into the water. They came up to the surface, treading water, to find themselves staring into the eyes of two large beavers. The other environmentalists were trying to balance their kayaks on the suddenly rough water while trying to rescue their two friends in the river. The beavers were very strong swimmers; one had started to pull the two who were in the water down and two other beavers who had joined the uproar began to capsize all the other kayaks. It didn't take long before all seven of the group were in the river, being attacked by four beavers. Grimes appeared to be the most fearful of the group, screaming "Get me out of here, Get me out, I've got to get out." He was being scratched and bitten as he was pulled down beneath the surface and away from the lodge as well as away from the shore. The other six had pulled their capsized kayaks over their heads for protection and were trying to get away from the lodge toward shore. They discovered it was very difficult as the network of brush and saplings underwater which helped to stabilize the lodge, became entangled with their legs, preventing an easy escape from the area. Grimes held on to his inverted kayak for some protection from the beavers, which gave him some buoyancy and speed in the current, taking him away from the lodge. As soon as the beavers stopped attacking him, he was able to aim straight for the shore to get on land again. He could see his friends still trying to defend themselves from the beavers, but didn't make any attempt to help them. He ran up to his SUV on the road to change into the clean, dry clothing he always kept in it. He shivered and felt panicky as he thought about all the river water he had swallowed and which had entered this body through the cuts and bites from the beavers.

It took well over a half hour for the six wet environmentalists to get to shore, defending themselves from the angry beavers and trying to free themselves from the intricate substructure of the lodge. They pulled their kayaks ashore, helping one another, exhausted and frightened by the unexpected attack. They looked around for Grimes but couldn't find him. One of the women had noticed him running from the shore, up toward the road. She told the others, and they all concurred that not making any attempt to rescue them, seemed like he abandoned them with no regard for their lives. They all felt fortunate to have evaded possible drowning and deadly attacks from the beavers. They sat on the shore, looking at the lodge, perched atop the river. The beavers who had attacked them were nowhere to be seen, but the sound of saplings crashing to the water could be heard again as the beavers returned to their work. As they rested on the shoreline waiting for Grimes to return, they debated what role, if any, he should have with any environmental coalition.

Grimes walked back to the group on the shore slowly. He was preoccupied with thoughts about how he would be affected by his own toxic formula. He was feeling irritable again. What had happened to his plan? Nothing seemed to be going his way. All he could think about was getting back home and taking a shower. He had to take some water samples from the river to analyze the concentration of his toxin. He knew the lodge was closer to the power plant, so it would likely have a higher concentration of the toxin than further down the river. But then, there was less sunlight in this area than further down the river and it was sunlight that activated the chemical to become genetically active, so maybe it was not as serious as he first considered it to be. Before he did anything else, he had to take these influential activists back to their hotel and then to the airport to meet their private plane which was scheduled to arrive in two hours.

"Where have you been? Why didn't you help us out there? We could have drowned," the man who was wearing the white hat with the green earth symbol on it asked. "I saw you run up the hill to get away. Look at you! You have clean dry clothes on, while we're still wet with cuts and bruises all over us", one of the women said. The six of them stared at Grimes, waiting for an answer. "I...I thought I saw someone on the road who could have helped," Grimes lied. "I don't believe you. We were just thinking that maybe you wouldn't be the appropriate spokesperson for our group or for those corporate consultancy positions we discussed. Get us out of here now! We have a plane to meet and have to get back to the ship. Do you think you're capable of doing that?" the man asked.

The group of environmentalists did not converse during the ride back to their hotel in Grimes' SUV. None of them spoke as they left him, walking into the lobby with their wet, torn clothing and bite and scratch marks on their arms, faces and legs. Their unusual appearances caused other guests and hotel staff to stare at them, causing greater embarrassment and anger to their already humiliating day. They agreed to get together, after showering and before their flight, to talk about their relationship with Grimes.

Chapter 41
Come This Way Please

After Grimes dropped the group off at the airport, he went home and showered, painfully scrubbing each scratch and bite on his body with soap, to be sure there was no residual river water in his wounds. He took with him some glass bottles for water samples from the river. The more he thought about the beavers attacking him and the environmentalists, he became infuriated with the beavers. He decided to go up to his abandoned farm where he kept his special coyotes and release them near the river. They would take care of those beavers and then just become part of the wildlife there. Now that Juice was no longer taking care of them, this was another opportunity for him to simplify his daily routine. He loaded the eight coyotes into the special transportation trailer and drove toward the river. He first took the water samples, and then drove further down a dirt road for added privacy. He didn't want anyone watching as he released the coyotes from the trailer. They bounded out of the trailer and quickly scattered across the woods, glad to be free from the confinement of the old barn.

Grimes was back on the state highway heading home, when he saw the red flashing lights of two state troopers' vehicles behind him, motioning him to pull over to the side of the road. He obediently pulled over, cursing under his breath at another inconvenience, while trying to maintain his composure to the four state troopers who were approaching his SUV. "Good afternoon, sir," the trooper closest to his vehicle said politely. "May I see your license and registration?" Grimes asked, "Why sure, here they are. What did I do that you pulled me over?" The trooper took his license over to his cruiser, while the other three stood around his SUV. It took less than five minutes before the first trooper walked back with his identification, saying "Mr. Grimes, we would like you to come with us to the barracks. There are some people there who would like to speak with you. We are arranging to have your vehicle towed to the barracks. We will transport you there in our cruiser. Come this way please." Grimes was not sure what was happening, but he knew that if he resisted, he would only make things worse for himself. He wondered if this involved some mistake Juice had made before he died, then wondered if Juice could still be alive. "All right. Before I talk to anybody, I want to speak with my lawyer first", Grimes answered.

Chapter 42
All Lawyered Up

Juice was lying in a special care unit of the hospital. He noticed he had some clear plastic tubing going from bags hanging on a pole next to his bed into his upper arm. He was less confused, but still had a pounding headache and dull throbbing in his injured leg. Two of his doctors came to tell him the condition of his leg had not improved and that he would need to have it amputated to prevent the infection from traveling to the rest of his body. He wished for a moment that this was part of a bad dream, and he would awaken to feel healthy again. But he knew this was really happening to him. The doctors asked him if he had a relative or someone who could be his healthcare proxy if there were complications with the surgery. "What's that? What do you mean?" Juice asked. "It's a formality we ask for everyone who has surgery. It means while you are unconscious in surgery or if you can't make your own decisions due to some complication after surgery, there would be someone you could trust who could make health-related decisions for you. It's for your own protection", the younger doctor replied with a forced smile, trying to appear cheerful. Juice was considering who he knew who could be this health-care proxy person and couldn't think of anyone. He had no relatives that he knew of, and didn't even know anyone who lived in his apartment building. There was only one human being he knew locally, and as he thought out loud, softly said "Thomas Grimes?" "What was that name? I want to be sure we understood what you said," the older doctor asked. Juice was sorry he mentioned Grimes' name. After all, Grimes never came back to help him. Could he trust him to make medical decisions for him? "Do you know how to contact your friend? We really need to get you to surgery before your condition gets more serious," the smiling doctor told him. Juice felt himself getting light-headed and groggy, and found himself saying Grimes' cell phone number. The doctors quickly wrote it down and gave it to the unit secretary to make the call.

When Grimes' phone rang, he was in the interview room at the State Police barracks. He read the caller ID on the phone, unwittingly made a face and decided not to answer it. The older detective noticed the caller ID was from a hospital, wrote the number down and gave it to the younger detective, nodding to him to call the number to find out if the call was an emergency for Grimes. The younger detective followed his instructions and dialed the number, identified himself, and said he was speaking for the recipient of the call. He asked if he could speak with the patient to see if he could help. Juice answered the phone and hesitantly told him he had worked for Grimes and didn't have anyone else to call to be his healthcare proxy before he had surgery.

The younger detective went back to the interview room, and asked Grimes, "Do you know someone who calls himself Juice? He wants to speak with you. He's in the hospital." Grimes turned his head away and refused to speak with Juice. He snapped his head back toward the younger detective and said, "I told you I'm not saying anything. You can just call my attorney and ask him."

Chapter 43
Violence & Death

The beavers had worked continuously building the new dam for the past 24 hours. Myrtle had brought in some raccoons to help. Some muskrats noticed all the activity and decided to help by dragging in some vegetation to plug some holes in the dam. They didn't know why the dam was being built so hastily, but could tell something important was going on because they had never seen so many beavers from different families working together. Just as the dam was finished, and the exhausted animals swam to the shore to rest, they heard a loud screech as four of Grimes' coyotes sprang from their hiding places among the brush on the shore. The combination of fatigue and total surprise to some of the beavers, raccoons and muskrats left them vulnerable to the attack. The ferocious coyotes tore at the animals savagely, destroying several and severely wounding many others. The stronger beavers, raccoons and muskrats jumped back into the river to escape the vicious predators who were unwilling to swim in the swift current. As the coyotes worked together surrounding other prey, they brutally attacked skunks and rabbits, leaving their lifeless bodies on the ground. The only sounds left were the whimpering's of the wounded animals, shivering in fear and pain.

Two of the coyotes left the carnage, running up the grassy hillside toward the road. They quickly caught the scent of more wildlife up near the big brick building. Slade, Violet, Opal, Soshi, Julian and the babies were still in their nest near the foundation of the building. They heard the howling of coyotes getting closer, and decided they would be easy prey if they stayed where they were. Slade suggested they go back to Soshi and Julian's warren to go underground for safety. The little group scurried to the now enlarged opening of the rabbit's burrow. Violet pushed the babies down the hole first and then told Opal to follow them. Soshi insisted that Violet go in next to take care of the babies and Opal. Surprisingly, Julian said he would go in last, after Soshi and Slade, and had no sooner dove in when two coyotes arrived. The tunnel's opening was very narrow for Violet and Slade, but Julian and Soshi pushed them down with all their strength. The opening which had caved in from the flood was much wider now, but the warren's interior narrowed quickly at the entrance of the tunnel toward the river.

Julian looked up from the tunnel to see the sharp canine teeth only inches away, snarling at him. The little group continued to push their way down the tunnel until safely away. The coyotes could only dig so far down the burrow before it started to cave in around them. They pulled back and began howling in rage at the hole for several minutes, disturbing the normally peaceful area. Maggie was in her window seat, watching in horror at the large coyotes hunting for prey where she usually walks with her mom.

Slade, Violet, Opal, Soshi, Julian and the babies finally made their way through the tunnel, with Soshi describing every turn, root system and rock along the way to guide them. He and Julian knew every inch of the tunnel by heart, as they had originally dug it together a few years ago. As they neared its end and could see the thick curtain of grass at the other opening, Soshi warned them to not eat any of the vegetation. They could hear more coyotes prowling and howling along the river's edge searching for more small prey. They had killed more rabbits and mink and were less aggressive for a while, but still in the area. Violet and Opal were trying to keep the babies quiet as they were unaware of the proximity of the coyotes and kept frolicking and rolling over each other, squeaking in the delight of their playfulness. The last thing they wanted was for the coyotes to detect their scent near the tunnel opening. Violet looked at her babies and thought that this is how it should be for baby muskrats: happy and innocent about life.

Chapter 44

Blood Lust

Myrtle, Abbie and Mr. Toad could hear that the coyotes' howling was getting closer to them. Myrtle told them to stay close to her and follow her up a tree where they would be safe. Abbie reminded her, "Wait! I can't climb a tree and neither can Mr. Toad. We need to get someplace else to be safe. Mr. Toad, start digging down next to that rock so they won't find you," Abbie frantically told him. "Don't worry, I will defend you, I'll never leave you," the toad said to Abbie. For the first time, Abbie realized these could be the last moments of her life. She never considered that being devoured by coyotes would be how her life would end. She thought about never seeing her mom, Maggie or Gabe again and as tears began to fall from behind her long lashes, she was startled by a loud screech from Myrtle's throat.

Within a minute, two large raccoons appeared before Myrtle, asking what was going on that was so urgent. Myrtle hurriedly said, "We need to start digging under that pile of rocks over there so this dog and toad can hide under them before those coyotes come here to attack them. I've never heard or seen coyotes as vicious before. I can climb up this tree, but they cannot," she told them. The three raccoons dug furiously to help Myrtle's friends, even though they had never met Abbie and Mr. Toad before. The hole didn't need to be very deep because the plan was to cover it with layers of large rocks. When the hole was about two feet deep, Myrtle said, "Get in, both of you, we're going to cover you with big rocks and tree limbs for protection." Abbie and Mr. Toad did what Myrtle told them to do. "We'll try to leave some space over your heads with the branches, but you will have to stay crouched down. There will be plenty of air for you to breathe." Abbie was impressed by the strength and dexterity the raccoons had as well as their ability to work together. "There's no one else who could be as efficient as a raccoon you know. Having three sets of thumbs working to save your life comes in handy," Myrtle reminded them. For the first time, Mr. Toad realized how right she was and whispered to Abbie, "I'll never complain about her bragging about the attributes of raccoons again."

Within minutes, the three raccoons had finished covering Abbie and Mr. Toad with a large pile of rocks. They turned around in time to see two very large coyotes rushing toward them. The three raccoons quickly climbed the tree over Abbie and Mr. Toad to safety and watched the predators pacing the ground where they had all stood just moments before. Myrtle noticed there was something different about these coyotes; not only were they much larger and more vicious, but they seemed to act as if in competition with one another. The coyotes' keen sense of smell immediately picked up the scent of Abbie and Mr. Toad under the pile of rocks. They howled loudly, and began to dig under the rocks, to expose their intended prey. Abbie and Mr. Toad huddled together, wondering if Gabe knew the peril they were in. The coyotes each dug independently of the other. One of the rocks had begun to fall away, exposing a small opening in the pile, revealing Abbie's face.

The coyotes became more aroused, pushing at the rock over Abbie's head to topple it away from her. Instead, the rock toppled onto one of the coyote's front paws, causing a trickle of blood to flow from it. The other coyote, noticed the blood immediately, and stopped digging at the rocks and began to attack its partner. A savage fight followed between the two coyotes. Abbie, Mr. Toad and the three raccoons watched in horror as the two animals viciously fought with one another. Finally after one had become so injured and fatigued, its partner tore into it one final time to cause a fatal wound. The victorious animal began to consume what had been its partner less than an hour before. After what seemed like an eternity to Abbie and Mr. Toad, the animal finally was satiated, leaving the remains of its prey on the ground and slowly walked away. Abbie and Mr. Toad breathed a sigh of relief, still trembling together and grateful to still be alive.

Chapter 45

A New Fear

The beavers had finally completed the dam to control the flow of water, creating a stationary pool of water contained by the debris carefully placed by the team. They avoided going on the shore to escape the coyotes and decided to all stay in Varun's lodge, even though they were from other beaver families. This was the first time they had all worked together as a group and with muskrats, helping to protect their habitats from further damage. They spoke about some of the changes they had all seen on the river and what Beryl had told them about what had happened to her own owl eggs. "We won't know for sure if the dam will change the current long enough to prevent that stuff from contaminating the water, but at least it will slow its spread. There are a lot of animals who depend on the river for water and shelter," Varun said. As they all sat around the lodge, crowded together, one of Varun's kits awakened and started to cry out loud. The beaver visitors turned to stare at the kit, shocked to see how small its tail was and that it had no teeth yet. How could a beaver not have teeth? How could it survive on its own? Suddenly one of the beaver guests thought out loud, saying "We were all in the water building the new dam, what's going to happen to us now?"

Chapter 46
Under Arrest

Grimes' SUV was lowered off the tow truck at the State Police crime lab building. Lab technicians approached it with HazMat protective clothing, masks and special gloves. They carefully took air samples from the interior of the vehicle, finger prints and removed the carpeting from the driver and passenger areas and then from the cargo area. Everything was carefully labelled and placed in special sealed bags to prevent contamination from and to the contents. They returned to the lab and began analyzing each sample. Several hours later, one of the chemists printed out a list of the compounds found in the various areas of the SUV. The list was very comprehensive, with most of the samples being commonly found in most vehicles. The two exceptions were unusual and questionable samples: an excess of coyote fur and the exact chemical found in the containers at the hydroelectric plant. The head chemist emailed his report labeled "Priority", to the older detective who was in his office with other detectives. He had left Grimes alone with his attorney, as he had demanded. The detective jumped up and said, "Let's go tell Grimes he is under arrest. He'll really need that attorney now with what we've found."

Grimes was charged with Environmental Terrorism. His bail was set and his attorney completed the necessary paperwork for his release on bail. He went home that night exhausted by a day of interrogation and worries about his own exposure to his toxin. He had a fitful sleep with numerous dreams. The most disturbing dream took place right before dawn. In it a shabbily dressed man with a fishing rod spoke to him about a place that could heal the effects of his harmful toxin if he was remorseful for his actions. Grimes told the man he had used sunlight to create his genetic changes and they were irreversible. He laughed heartily at the man in the dream, and awakened to find himself laughing out loud at the foolishness of his dream.

Chapter 47

Compassion

Juice had his eyes closed, waiting for the hospital to hear from Grimes about agreeing to be his POA for the surgery. He was thinking about the events of the past several days, unsure what had actually happened. He felt groggy from the medications he was given and still had a pounding headache. He heard someone enter his room and opened his eyes. He saw the shabbily dressed man who had been at the river now standing in his room. The man simply said, "Hello. I will be your Healthcare Proxy if you would like." Juice replied, "Huh? How did you know? Why would you do this for me?" The man answered "I happened to be here at the hospital and overheard you needed someone to help you out." Juice stared at the man for the first time, really looking beyond his clothes and into his eyes. There was a kindness there that he had never before seen and felt a sense of peacefulness and acceptance. He noticed that although his clothing was worn and tattered, it was clean and his appearance was flawless. "Why would you do this for me?" Juice asked. The man replied, "Because you need help right now to get the surgery without any more delays. Your friend Grimes chose to not help you." "I don't even know your name," Juice said to him. "My name is Raphael." Juice agreed to let Doc Ray be his proxy. Within the hour he was in surgery for the amputation.

Chapter 48
Unconditional Love

Myrtle and her raccoon friends descended the tree quickly to begin uncovering Abbie and Mr. Toad from the rocky shelter they had built to protect them from the coyotes. Mr. Toad hopped out first, not wanting to have any of the rocks roll onto his little body and crush him. Abbie crawled out a minute later, covered with sand and sneezing to get the dirt out of her little nose. She stared at the coyote carcass in front of them as testament of its vicious fight with the other coyote. "Are you all right? I've never seen anything so scary in all my life. Those coyotes were huge!" Myrtle exclaimed. Abbie and Mr. Toad were still shaking from the experience. "We never would have survived if you didn't help us," Abbie said to Myrtle. "I've never protected a dog before, but now that I've spent some time with you and your little friend here, you're kind of like family, even though you're not raccoons. It just felt like the right thing to do. We need to get back to the beavers and other raccoons at the lodge now," she said. "Let's go."

Myrtle, the two raccoons, and Abbie with Mr. Toad on her shoulders hastily set out to find out if the beavers had completed their new dam. They crossed the bridge of branches and saplings on the river and noticed that the flow of water was barely moving. The depth of water before the dam was now quite deep. They were able to cross over to the top of the lodge in hopes that one of the beavers would hear them and show them how to enter the lodge from the upper surface. Varun was the first to detect movement on the roof of the lodge and came out to investigate. "Oh, it's you. Come on down but be careful where you walk to not to break anything," he said. They did as they were told and found themselves inside the lodge. It was quite crowded and dark, with a strong odor of beaver musk. Abbie found it offensive and started to sniffle again and almost shook Mr. Toad off her shoulders several times from sneezing so hard.

"We were just saying how worried we are now that we've all been exposed to that stuff in the water," Varun stated. "Beryl is quite angry at the man that she saw put the chemical in the water. Her baby owls had died as a result of his actions." Abbie and Mr. Toad understood their anger. She whispered to him, "I wish Gabe were here, I don't know what to say." Suddenly there was a small sparkle of light that expanded into Gabe's wonderful presence. "Gabe!" Abbie cried out. The lodge was instantly filled with light that was both soft and intense at the same time. Abbie instinctively moved closer to Gabe, as the mixed beaver odors were not as overwhelmingly strong next to him. "I thought I'd drop in to see how things were going. I've been told to let you know the Creator is very pleased with the way you've all worked together to overcome the evil that was done to your environment. The dam that you beavers made will slow down the water flow so that the toxin will sink to the bottom and become harmless without sunlight. It won't be a danger to any lifeforms anymore. The person who invented this toxin wanted to use energy from the sunlight, thinking he would be a "creator" of new living things. He wanted to subvert the natural benefits of sunlight for his own purposes. What he didn't count on was your recognition that by working together his terrible plan could be obstructed," Gabe explained.

"That's all well and good, but what about my kits?" Varun asked angrily. "They will be lucky to survive, they'll never be able to live a normal beaver's life. And what about us? We were all working in that water for hours on end, we don't know how that will affect our lives." There was a cacophony in the lodge from all the adult beavers agreeing with Varun. Suddenly, the cries of the deformed, baby beavers rang out, silencing the adults. All eyes turned to their misshapen bodies. Gabe said, "These babies are the result of a person's hatefulness and pride. Going against the natural order of Creation can only lead to destruction and chaos. But look at what just happened. In their cries, they just captured your attention. You all know they need more help because of what has happened to them. Their bodies are not a perfect beaver body. They will need more help than their natural parents can provide for them. One of the larger males at the back of the lodge called out, "I'd be willing to help Varun and his wife with these kits. They might never be able to swim on their own, but I have strong shoulders, and I'm a good swimmer. I'll take them for a ride down the river." All the rest of the beaver guests in the lodge loudly agreed and promised to help feed and take care of them. Varun and his wife shared a thankful glance at each other as a beaver guest went over to one of the male babies and ruffled up the fur on his neck as a sign of affection. The kit looked up at him with big brown eyes and nuzzled his head against the adult's furry arm.

Gabe looked around at the animals and said, "Unfortunately, the genetic effects of the toxin on these babies and other species already damaged are permanent, and reminders that the natural order of life is not to be manipulated. Varun, your children and the other affected animals will serve to enlighten humans that they must not tamper with natural creation. Don't worry, they will no longer be harmed in any way. As for all of you who have been exposed to the toxin, a good friend of mine has the anti-toxin that will prevent any harm from exposure before damage begins. "You mean there's no danger to us then?" a middle-aged female beaver asked. "By choosing to care and help one another, you share in the Creator's Unconditional Love and healing," Gabe answered. "You have risked your own lives for the lives of others you didn't even know. This kind of love opens your hearts to the real Truth of living the purposeful life that is the Creator's plan. My friend is waiting for you downstream near the shore. You can't miss him, he's standing near that big rock overlooking the river."

Mr. Toad and Myrtle breathed a sigh of relief. Abbie didn't dare take any more breaths than she had to due to the stuffiness and musky smells of the lodge. Gabe turned to them and said, "Time to go. There's much more we need to do yet."

Chapter 49
The Vine

Maggie was barking wildly at the coyotes from her third floor window seat, which caused her mom to come and see what the commotion was all about. She typically was a very quiet Shih Tzu who only barked when the doorbell rang. Her mom saw the two large coyotes howling and excitedly digging into a widening hole in the ground. She had never seen coyotes so large or close to the building before and became concerned for the safety of people and dogs who frequent the area. She decided to call the local Animal Control officer to report the presence of the unusually vicious coyotes. The officer said he would be on his way and at the building within a half hour.

The coyotes at the river had separated from their group. Three scavenged the area for any animals that had been injured but were still alive, looking to senselessly kill them. They were not interested in them as a source of food but only to act out more violence on the helpless creatures. Another coyote wandered up toward the new beaver dam again, and the fifth one wandered aimlessly toward the road above the river.

About thirty minutes later, the animal control officer arrived at the building, having no trouble finding the noisy coyotes. He was well-prepared and knew the potential danger of two or more coyotes to humans. He had a tranquilizer weapon, which he expertly fired first at one and then the other animal to render them temporarily harmless. Within two minutes, they both sleepily fell to the ground, enabling him to muzzle them and place them in the cages in his truck. He was rather surprised at the size and muscle mass of the animals, wondering if these were a different breed of coyote. It was unusual that they would be so vicious and so close to a building inhabited by so many people. He drove away with Maggie still watching from her window seat above.

Violet and Opal were unsuccessfully trying to keep the babies from squirming and sweaking in the narrow tunnel. They were energetic and at the age where they liked to roll over one another and playfully chase each other until they would cuddle together and drop off to sleep. Slade was losing patience with them after they repeatedly would jump on his belly. They figured out if they used his belly as a springboard, they could roll over one another more forcefully. Julian was the one who noticed Slade's annoyance, and motioned to the babies to follow him up the tunnel to the next turn where they would be further away from the opening and from Slade. Soshi followed them and watched delightedly at how Julian's attitude was changing. He was becoming more loving and less grumpy and seemed to be more tolerant and protective of Soshi and his new friends. Maybe all these changes would result in a brand new life for them. Even in the midst of danger a few yards away, Soshi could sense a peacefulness in the little group.

Opal was close enough to the tunnel's opening to smell the death and destruction and hear the sounds of the two coyotes tearing into wounded animals. She shuddered at the thought of the suffering on the riverbank. Tears welled up in her golden-brown eyes. Violet noticed her sadness and fear and pushed her wide body over to Opal, placing an arm around the little rabbit to console her. "Why is this happening? Why is there so much killing and destruction going on? What did these animals ever do to deserve being killed for no reason?"

Opal sobbed into Violet's thick coat. She was sure she had no surviving rabbit family. Her parents, siblings, cousins, aunts and uncles all lived by the river in what they had believed was a reasonably safe area. "Now, now, I can't answer those questions about why this is happening. You are young, and this is the first time you are experiencing something really bad in our life. I truly hope it will be the last time for you. But I can promise you that you have a new family now. Slade and I, Soshi and Julian, and the babies, we're all in this together, helping one another and growing stronger together. Isn't that what families are supposed to do?" Violet asked Opal. "Yes, it is, but we're not out of this tunnel yet. We don't know how many threats are still out there, waiting to harm us too. I couldn't bear to see anything happen to those babies," Opal whimpered. Violet answered, "But we never know what threats await us in life. The best we can ever do is live with the skills we are born with and take care of our family and friends. Sometimes bad things happen, but we can't let those bad things ruin our lives. They will, if we choose to give the memories of those bad experiences that much power over us."

"You see, life itself is like a big, very special vine that can provide all of us with what we need to live. Now a person can look at that big vine and decide they don't like something about it. Maybe where it is, maybe the kind of nourishment that grows on it, maybe they feel it provides more for others than it does for themselves. They can get mad at the vine and decide to try and find another vine someplace else that will give them what they want. But what they don't realize is *they* are a small part of that vine *themselves*. By choosing to leave the vine, they only hurt themselves by severing themselves from the vine. Focusing on our disappointments and hurt in life is like slowly separating ourselves from the vine, each day receiving less goodness from it. When it seems like the vine is not providing what we think it should, our trust in the vine is diminished. We need to make sure our attachment to it has not been weakened by losing trust in it."

Opal took her head out of Violet's dense brown fur, leaving a dent of wet, matted fur where her head was buried. "Will you show me how to have some confidence in the vine? I think I need that after what has happened around here," the little rabbit asked. "Oh, Opal, of course I will," Violet said.

Chapter 50
Do The Right Thing

Gabe, Abbie and Mr. Toad left the beaver lodge, although Abbie couldn't remember just how they left the lodge with Gabe. She realized that somehow Gabe fit into the compact lodge, whose height was adequate for the animals, but not for a human. But somehow, he was standing with them, looking like his perfect, sparkling self. It was too much to comprehend, because the next thing she knew, she and Gabe and Mr. Toad were back at the red brick building. They looked up to a third floor window at Maggie, still staring down where the coyotes had been. When she saw Abbie, her bark changed. She noticed that Abbie had a toad on her shoulders, and was accompanied by someone she had never seen before.

Gabe looked up at Maggie and asked Abbie, "Isn't Maggie's dad in law enforcement?" Abbie said, "I don't know, I never asked Maggie where her dad went to work. Why?" Gabe answered, "It would be very nice if the person who caused all this damage could be held accountable. Do you think she would be interested in helping us with that? We could pay her a visit, when she is alone," Gabe explained. Mr. Toad was a little apprehensive about having a dog he didn't know as part of their group. He had seen Maggie before, and she seemed a little too interested in investigating a toad. Maybe that was because her dad was in law enforcement he thought. Abbie said, "Sure, we're good friends. But how can she help?" Gabe explained, "We need to allow the appropriate consequences to unfold, so that the person who wanted to modify natural life for his own self-interests will never be able to cause any more damage."

Abbie and Mr. Toad instantaneously found themselves in Maggie's apartment. She was alone, her mom had gone out after the coyotes were taken away. "How did you get in here? What happened to you? I've never seen you without your pigtails," Maggie asked Abbie, shocked to see her hair so messy. "It's a long story, but we need your help with something," Abbie responded. "You should have been here a little while ago. There were two huge coyotes right under my windows. It's a good thing I saw them from my seat. I wouldn't stop barking until my mom came over to see what the fuss was all about. They're gone now. The animal police took them away. They were near where we walk with our moms. It's safe now." Abbie shook her head, body and tail, spraying sand all over the clean carpeting. "Hey, don't do that! Tracey just finished cleaning everything," Maggie reprimanded Abbie.

Mr. Toad was about to laugh, but thought better about that, not knowing how Maggie would respond to him. Before Abbie could apologize, Gabe appeared, unfolding into his beautiful, luminous self. Maggie was about to run and hide, but found her little legs wouldn't move, so she stood there like a Shih Tzu statue, with her mouth slightly open. "Hi, Maggie," Gabe said to her. "It's all right, I would never hurt you. We would like to ask for your help with something." Abbie chimed in, "His name is Gabe, isn't he wonderful?" Maggie finally found her voice again and said, "But why me?" "Since your dad is an officer of the law, you can help him get some very important information that he wouldn't be able to have without your help," Gabe replied. "We'll take you to see someone who can give you that information." Maggie thought for a moment. Abbie interrupted her thoughts and said, "Listen, have you ever seen me so messy before? Do you think I would let myself get like this if it wasn't important? When everything is all done, we'll explain what it's all about. We can trust Gabe, believe me." "OK, I guess. What do I tell my mom. I never go out without her. Won't she wonder where I am?" Maggie asked.

The next thing Maggie knew, she was with Gabe, Abbie and the toad, and in a bright room someplace else. Gabe was standing behind a curtain in the room, with Abbie and Mr. Toad on one shoulder, and Maggie on the other. They looked down at a man in a bed who had some tubes going into his arms that were connected to some little bags hanging on a pole next to his bed. He looked like he was sleeping, but seemed to be mumbling some words.

"I remember him, he's the guy who trapped Soshi, Dustin and Selena. He talked about not having his father around when he was growing up," Mr.

Toad said. "As I remember, you found you had something in common with him, which made you feel uncomfortable," Gabe said. "So what happened to him? He looks even worse than when we saw him the last time," Mr. Toad said. Gabe explained, "Well, because he let his anger control his actions, he fell on his own hunting knife when he was trying to harm someone else and severely injured his own leg. The injury was so serious, it resulted in him having to have that leg amputated and that is why he is here in a hospital now. He is not fully awake yet, that's why he is mumbling. He'll be all right in the end, but he has a lot of healing to do, first with his mind and then with his body." Abbie and Maggie both cringed at the thought of having a leg amputated. It was bad enough just having the groomer trim their nails, let alone have a leg cut off. Just then, a nurse came up to Juice and appeared to be checking him and looking at various computer screens that were monitoring his condition through the tubes and wires attached to him.

Gabe said, "The nurses who are taking care of this guy can't see or hear us, so when we speak to him, they will only be able to hear him speak, not us. Maggie, I would like you to ask him about the coyotes you saw outside of your window. Because he is semi-conscious now, he will be able to answer your questions." "I've never seen anyone look so sick before," Maggie said. "Are you sure he can understand dog language?" "Normally he wouldn't be able to, but right now, his mind is in a, let's say, fluid state," Gabe explained.

Maggie jumped on the bed and carefully walked over to his shoulder, and said near Juice's ear, "Do you know why there were two huge coyotes near where I live? They were really big and mean, and looked like they were trying to find something to eat." Juice slowly turned his head toward Maggie's little seven pound body, opened his eyes and said, "Wha.....Who are you? You're a dog, you're talking to me, dogs aren't supposed to talk. Where am I?" "You're in a hospital," Mr. Toad chimed in. He had hopped on the bed, standing on Juice's chest. "Remember me? We talked once before when you were on your couch." Juice's eyes both opened very wide, like he couldn't believe what he seeing and hearing. "Get away from me! You're not real, you can't be real! Help! Help!" Juice yelled out loud. "I only asked you a question, just tell me about the really big coyotes outside the big red building and we'll leave you alone," Maggie said.

Juice glared at the little dog with a combination of fright and frustration. Two nurses ran to Juice's bedside, responding to the alarms that went off when he was yelling for help. "It's OK, there's nothing to be afraid of," one nurses told him. The other nurse muttered under her breath, "It's probably just post-operative psychosis, and he lost a lot of blood. He might be agitated for awhile. He might need some Haldol if he gets worse. We'll have to keep a close watch on this one."

Maggie and Mr. Toad had not moved from their positions. Mr. Toad looked down at Juice from his big, bulgy toad eyes. Maggie repeated, "Just tell me why the big coyotes were near my windows and we'll leave you alone." The two nurses remained near the foot of Juice's bed. Abbie and Gabe were standing next to the nurses, but were not visible to them. "The coyotes are part of Grimes' project. He used them as experiments for his secret formula. Part of my job was to feed them everyday for two years. There were eight pups when I trapped them, just a few weeks old. He wouldn't let me skin them, said he had better plans for them. I would drive up to that abandoned farm every day to feed them raw meat the supermarkets would give me, you know meat that had gone past the expiration date. I would mix his special formula in their drinking water. Grimes called it their vitamin water. I don't know what was in it, but it made them grow very big and very mean. Even I was afraid of getting too close to them."

"I don't know how they got out of the barn where we kept them. I don't know why they were near your window. They weren't supposed to get out, they were dangerous. He promised me I could skin them and sell their pelts when the experiment was over." Gabe said, "Maggie, tell him your dad's name and where he works, insist he needs to tell the nurses about the coyotes and to get in touch with your dad. Tell him he needs to tell the truth to help himself and to make things right." Abbie looked at Maggie and said, "Please do as Gabe asked. I'll explain everything when we get back home. It's the right thing to do now." Maggie thought about the eight coyote pups who were taken from their mother and used as an experiment for two years.

She bent over toward Juice's ear and said, "Don't you think enough damage has been done already? For once in your life, do the right thing and you tell those nurses or someone here, you know what you're saying and you want to talk to my dad. I'll tell you his name and where he works." "OK, OK. Then you and the toad will leave me alone, right?" Juice asked.

"Time for you to get back home, Maggie, before your mom does. You did a great job! Time for all of us to go," Gabe said to Abbie, Mr. Toad and Maggie. In an instant, Maggie found herself back at home, on her window seat, wondering if she had just awakened from a very realistic dream, until she noticed the little pile of dirt on the floor where Abbie had been standing.

The nurses decided to call in the psychologist to evaluate Juice's condition again for delirium. His opinion was that Juice was not delirious or psychotic, and did not require any antipsychotic medications. He carried out Juice's insistence to contact Maggie's dad, who said he would follow-up with the request the next day.

Chapter 51
Credence Rock

A heavy fog had rolled in during the late afternoon, almost concealing Doc Ray among the shrubs and tall grasses along the river bank. He was leaning against a very large rock, that was near a honeybee hive. The coolness of the fog had made the bees less active so they lazily buzzed around the hive laden with the pollen they had gathered from nearby wildflowers. Suddenly a ray of sunlight shone on the damp rock attracting the bees to swarm on it and deposit their pollen on its surface. Doc Ray smiled at the bees, saying to them, "You have behaved as you were created to behave. Protect this rock and the creatures who visit it for healing in good faith. From now on, it will be called Credence Rock." Within minutes the sunlit rock was covered in moist pollen that had become a sweet, sticky coating. He looked up, hearing the sounds of breaking twigs from some running animals. His eyes met those of two coyotes that were on their way up to the new beaver dam.

The animals looked rabid, although they were not. They were panting heavily, sniffing the ground for fresh scents. They glanced at Doc Ray, who did not make a move toward them. The animals crouched to the ground and growled at him. They started to crawl near the rock, snarling at him, baring sharp, large teeth. Suddenly the entire hive erupted, with thousands of bees swarming over and stinging the coyotes. They howled in pain and confusion, spinning around and running away, trying to outrun the bees. The animals tried to rub the bees off of their bodies, but as they howled, more bees flew into their mouths, stinging their throats. Within minutes, they dropped to the ground, unable to breathe as their windpipes were too swollen to allow for the passage of air. The bees left the lifeless animals where they had dropped, and returned to the hive.

Varun, Myrtle, the beavers, raccoons and other animals who had worked on the dam saw Doc Ray at the rock. They had come upon the dead coyotes and were frightened that there would be new dangers awaiting them. He welcomed them, motioning that it was safe for them to proceed. Varun asked, "You are Gabe's friend? We have all been exposed to the toxin in the river and are hopeful you are able to heal us from its harmful effects." Doc Ray answered, "Yes, I am his friend. Yes, the healing you seek is here at this rock that is now called 'Credence Rock'. It will heal you and others who approach it as long as you have truth and love for others in your hearts. Do not be afraid, because your Faith in the Creator's unconditional love will protect you from harm. Come and taste its sweetness." Varun and the others warily approached the rock, smelling it first, then touching it lightly, and then licking its honeyed coating. When they all had their fill of the pleasant flavor, Doc Ray said to them, "I must be leaving here. Please let your families and friends know of Credence Rock if they have been exposed to the toxin. All are welcome to come here and take their fill of the healing powers of the Creator." With this, Doc Ray bid them all good-bye and walked into the woods until they could no longer see him through the saplings and bushes.

Chapter 52
In This Together

Gabe led the way, with Mr. Toad on Abbie's shoulders to find Slade, Violet, Soshi, Julian, Opal and the baby muskrats. Abbie stopped short, catching the scent of blood from the carcasses of small animals along the river. "This is awful! I've never seen anything like this and hope I never will again. I don't want to go any further." She stopped so short that Mr. Toad was almost thrown off her head. His sticky hands grabbed what was left of her pigtails, pulling her ears over her eyes. She instinctively went into a whole body-shake, that caught him off guard, causing him to fall onto the ground. Gabe immediately picked him up, and then Abbie, as she had taken one of her famous land anchor positions, standing stiff-leggedly and refusing to walk.

"We need to keep going, I know it's hard for you, but your friends are kind of in a tough spot right now. There are still three coyotes left in the area." "What happened to the others?" Mr. Toad asked. Gabe explained, "Well, there were eight of them. Two were taken away by local animal control officers, one was killed by one of its own, two others were stung to death by some bees. So there are still three that need to be found before this area can be safe again." "It seems like this is never going to end. I just want to be home again, and get a bath, although I never thought I would say that, and sleep in bed again, where everything is safe," Abbie said. She was becoming sulky and irritable with all the destruction and death. "Hey, now stop a minute and look at what's happened so far," Gabe said. "I don't want to stop and look, it's too…too much," Abbie said, bursting into tears.

Mr. Toad looked across from Gabe's right shoulder to his left shoulder, where Abbie was perched. "But we chose to do this because it was the right thing to do, not because it was the easy thing to do," he said to her. For the first time, he stretched out his long tongue toward her face and gave her a toadly kiss, sweeping it from one cheek, over her tiny nose to the other cheek. "But I'm here with you. We're in this together, remember?" he said to her. "And besides, Gabe is with us. He'll protect us." Gabe stopped and asked, "Is that what you think I'm here for?" "Well, aren't you?" Mr. Toad asked him. "I told you I am a messenger, that is my purpose," he explained. Gabe continued on the path, carrying Abbie on one shoulder, and Mr. Toad sitting on the other. They had noticed the fog growing heavier and were glad they were being carried. The air seemed much thicker now and the sky had become quite dark, even though it was not yet nightfall.

Chapter 53
Selfless

Julian had been playing with the babies inside the tunnel to occupy their time and help them burn off some of their energy. He was so successful, that he and the babies had fallen asleep against one another in a big, furry hump. They were up higher in the tunnel so that their antics would not be heard near the tunnel's lower opening. What Julian had forgotten was that they were near another exit of the tunnel that was about midway down the hillside. It was well designed and camouflaged by Soshi so that they could easily exit in an emergency. What he was not aware of was that one of the coyotes heard the ruckus of him playing with the babies. Their squeaks of delight signaled tender, easy prey for the vicious predator. It did not take him long to dig away the rocks covering the bend in the tunnel, and stick his long snout into the opening and begin howling.

Julian and the babies awoke at once, feeling the flow of air and seeing the remaining daylight enter the tunnel. He gathered them away and pushed them further down toward the river, where the others were. "Soshi! Are there any other exits you may have made in this tunnel? There is a coyote ready to burst in up there. It's not safe anymore! What should we do?" Julian asked him. The babies were now crying, and had huddled under Violet's arms. Opal looked panic-stricken at Violet, ready to cry again. "I guess I need to poke my head out and see if anything is outside of the tunnel's river opening," Soshi said. He slowly moved toward the exit and noticed it had begun to rain quite heavily. He hopped out carefully, looking around, afraid of what he would find. Julian followed him out. "I'm sorry for everything I've put you through, of always putting myself first, and having you be the one to take care of everything. It was wrong. I see now that truly caring about others actually makes a person happier than always putting yourself first."

Julian had barely finished talking when a large coyote had pounced on his back, grabbing him by the neck with his sharp teeth. Julian screamed in pain and surprise as he was being dragged away from the tunnel's opening, right in front of Soshi. Slade came running out to see what had happened. Soshi didn't think twice and ran after Julian and his predator, grabbing the animal's tail with his front teeth and biting down as hard as he could. But the tail had such a thick coat, he only ended up with a mouthful of fur. He continued hopping as fast as he could, following Julian, but the rabbit's speed was no match for coyote speed. The rain was torrential now, falling in heavy sheets, with lightening flashing all around them and huge claps of thunder simultaneous with the lightening. Soshi had never seen a storm as severe before. Visibility was down to just a few feet in front of him, but he continued to follow the scent of the coyote, intent on rescuing Julian, even if it meant harm to himself.

The sound Julian's cries were heard by the remaining two coyotes which were nearby. They raced toward the sounds of an injured animal which would be easy prey. Picking up his scent from being dragged on the ground as well as Soshi's scent, the two mutated coyotes yelled in tandem, becoming even more vicious, preparing to devour another victim. The coyote carrying Julian stopped running and dropped Julian to the ground and turned around. Soshi was still hopping as fast as he could in pursuit, and suddenly found himself staring into the large, sinister eyes of the snarling coyote. Soshi stared back in anger, and for a moment, they just stayed there together, the huge predator glowering down at the rabbit. They were both startled when they saw two more coyotes bearing down on them. The coyote who had been dragging Julian crouched down, ready to jump up and defend himself and his prey from their intended attack. Soshi recognized his one chance to save Julian, who lay on the ground panting and unable to move. He hopped over to him and pushed his body into some tall grass away from the melee of three coyotes. He thought at the very least, if they were to be devoured, they would both die together. The pounding rain continued, diluting the blood from Julian's wounds to pink as it flowed into the earth. Soshi noticed he was shivering from shock and still had not tried to move a muscle. The sounds of the three coyotes fighting just a few feet away made Soshi realize that even though there was something unnatural about their viciousness, he was able to stare down one of them out of love for Julian.

Suddenly, between the flashes of lightning and crashes of thunder, Soshi thought he saw something suspended in the air, moving away from Julian and him toward the coyotes. It was then Soshi realized what he thought was thunder and lightning were actually streaks of light and energy coming from what looked like the sword of someone flying through the air. It was hard to say what the figure was, looking like a very bright light with no substantive body, but still having some shape to it. The thing that resembled a sword gleamed in a brilliance Soshi had never before seen, crashing down on the coyotes, one by one. It was over as quickly as it had begun. The magnificence and speed of the thing that had wielded such power was gone, leaving the remains of the three coyotes lifeless on the ground.

"Julian! Look at me, can you hear me?" Soshi pleaded with his friend. Julian's eyes were half closed, the wounds on his neck still bleeding into the soil. The rain had abruptly stopped, but the two rabbits were soaked to their skins. "I'm so cold," Julian responded softly, "I can't stop shaking." "We need to get away from here. Can you walk?" Soshi asked him. "I don't think so, don't worry about me, you need to keep yourself safe," Julian murmured. "I'm not leaving you alone," Soshi insisted. "What if more coyotes come? They'll smell my blood. Then you'll be killed too," Julian said weakly. Soshi thought he heard footsteps coming toward them, but not four-footed steps. "Here you are, I knew you would be waiting," Gabe said. He bent over so that Abbie and Mr. Toad could jump down and see the two rabbits. Abbie had to look away from the awful gaping holes through Julian's brown fur exposing his wounds. "Who did this?" she asked. Gabe said, "More of those coyotes, but they're all gone now, there aren't any left. We have to get you healed before you lose more blood. Soshi, Abbie and Mr. Toad, you can all follow me. I'm going to carry Julian now because he can't walk on his own."

Gabe gently picked the injured rabbit up and began to walk up the river. Julian was still trembling, but noticed he felt completely safe in Gabe's arms and didn't have any more pain. He glanced into Gabe's eyes and felt the love he had for him and all life on earth, without him ever having to use words. Within minutes, they arrived at Credence Rock. There was a line of various animals there who all lived near or on the river. They looked up when they saw Gabe carrying Julian, recognizing the severity of his injuries and they instinctively moved away from the rock so he could be brought up to it. Gabe gently placed Julian on the ground next to Credence Rock and said to him, "I know you are very weak, but if you believe that all these animals are your fellow creatures and you will live according to the ways that rabbits were created to live, you will be healed if you place your tongue on this rock." Soshi, Mr. Toad and the line of other animals remained silent, watching and waiting. Abbie stood by with tears in her eyes, staring at Julian's broken body.

Julian looked up at Gabe smiling at him and knew he could trust him. He slowly pulled himself toward the large rock and extended his tongue to it. The effort used every last ounce of strength he had. His head toppled over his shoulders, as his neck muscles were damaged from the attack, and he fell over on his side, panting heavily. "Julian!" Soshi screamed. Mr. Toad slowly hopped over to him, as they were now, literally, eye to eye. He thought about the first time he had met Julian in his warren near the big red brick building. Now, he was almost lifeless and still slowly bleeding. The differences between toads and rabbits didn't seem to matter anymore, just that they both shared the animal kingdom together. Mr. Toad felt overwhelming sadness, his long tongue swept across Julian's cheek. He realized this was something he had learned from Abbie. She said it was a "kiss" and this was how dogs showed someone they cared about them. As he stood next to Julian's face on the ground, Julian opened his eyes, his whiskers stood out straight, and his ears went upright. The wounds on his neck started to close and heal. Everyone watched in amazement at the healing that was occurring right before their eyes. Julian turned to Abbie and said, "Sorry about all those rude things I said about dogs. I never really thought you smelled that bad at all."

Chapter 54
Sweet Partings

Gabe informed everyone at Credence Rock that the dangers from the coyotes had ended. He encouraged them to tell all their families, friends and neighbors to visit the rock's healing powers if they were exposed to the toxin in the water. More importantly, they must respect one another and the environment that was given to them by the Creator. Everyone clapped after hearing Gabe speak, and they slowly lined up again to have their turn at Credence Rock. Abbie asked Gabe, "Should Mr. Toad and I lick the Rock too? We were in the river water." "Well, I really need to get you both back home, and I need to move on myself. When you are back home, I have something that Doc Ray gave me for the two of you. You might want to say good-bye to some of the friends you've made here before you go," Gabe said. "Wait, wait, what do you mean say good-bye? Like I'll never see Myrtle or Violet or Opal or any of the others again?" Mr. Toad asked. "Probably not. You don't live outside anymore, remember? You live with Abbie in the apartment."

Mr. Toad thought for a moment, wondering what to do. He had grown to love Abbie and wanted to share his life with her. But since this whole adventure began, he had to admit he rather enjoyed meeting new friends, and there was always the endless variety of bugs near the river. Gabe knew what he was thinking, and said, "But what would you do in the winter, when there aren't any bugs flying around? You would have to dig deeply into the earth and be totally alone for months." Mr. Toad reflected on this, and thought about all the other things that Abbie had promised to teach him when they were alone during the day. "OK, you're right. But you said we'll have a chance to say good-bye, right?" Gabe laughed and said, "Yes, I did. Abbie, are you ready to go?" "Yes, I miss my mom and bed and I need a bath, which is something I never thought I would say."

Slade, Violet, Opal and the babies had ventured out of the tunnel, sniffing around the shoreline. Violet had to keep the baby muskrats away from the remains of the animals killed by the coyotes. Slade looked up to see Soshi and Julian both hopping over to them. "Oh, I was afraid I would never see you two again," Violet said joyfully. Opal ran up to them, hugging first Soshi and then Julian. Myrtle, Dustin and Selena came scampering down the hillside toward them, with Dustin licking the remains of pizza from his long fingernails. "You would not believe what we saw up near that building and down at the river: absolutely huge coyotes. I think the only animals capable of outwitting them are raccoons. You know, they were all brawn, but didn't look that smart if you ask me," she said. They all looked up at the shadow of an elegant owl flying above them. It was Beryl, scanning the treetops to make a new nest for the new eggs that she soon would lay. Opal said, "Isn't she beautiful?" Myrtle replied, "You wouldn't say that if she decided to have you for breakfast one day. You can trust raccoons. At least you know what you're dealing with when you deal with us."

Just then Gabe walked to where they were standing, along with Abbie and Mr. Toad. Myrtle said, "I was just telling them how helpful raccoons are. We might steal a few eggs when we get the chance, but we're good fishermen and don't swoop down and grab small animals for lunch." Mr. Toad shook his head so hard his tongue partially flew out of his mouth at hearing this. Abbie decided she would be the first to break the news she and Mr. Toad would be going home. When she opened her mouth to speak, tears rolled down from her eyes. "I'm going to miss you all, but I need to go back to my home. It's up there on the top floor of the big red brick building. I can look out and see all of this, I hope I can see you all too, but I don't think you would be able to see me." Myrtle replied, "I could climb up the big oak tree and wave to you. Raccoons are excellent climbers you know." "I would love that!" Abbie said. Mr. Toad stood there, rolling his eyes at Myrtle's boastfulness. "And you," Myrtle said to Mr. Toad, "I've never met a toad who was as handsome or smart or who knew how to read before!" At this, Mr. Toad decided maybe Myrtle wasn't as immodest as he had originally thought. After much hugging and promises to somehow meet again, Gabe picked up Abbie and Mr. Toad on his shoulders.

In an instantaneous swirl of brilliant light and air, they found themselves back in Abbie's apartment. Everything appeared as though nothing had changed. No one was at home. Gabe gently placed Abbie and Mr. Toad down on the floor. His aquarium was there with a fresh bowl of water in it. He was happy to see it and hopped over to it and down the rocks that led to his little sleeping spot over some moss. Abbie ran around checking out her food dish and to be sure the vacuum cleaner had not sucked up any of her favorite toys. Best of all, it smelled like home to her. She walked by a mirror and noticed she was clean, with fresh bows for her pigtails. She looked over to Gabe and was about to ask him how this happened, when he smiled and said, "I figured while we were enroute home, we could get you groomed."

Abbie was about to ask how his happened but knew that anything was possible with Gabe. They ran back over to him, seeing that he was waiting to say good-by to them. He had something in his hand that smelled like peanut butter. "If you would like, I have this from Doc Ray to heal you in case you have any of the toxin in your bodies. He opened his hand so they could both lick the substance Doc Ray had prepared for them. Abbie then jumped up on his leg and began to cry. She had become accustomed to him being in her life and now the thought of being without his perfection was startlingly heartbreaking. "Will we ever see you again? I can't bear the thought of not having you in my life," she said. "Well, little one, you are the most special Shih Tzu I've ever met. I can promise you two things: first, I am always with you whenever you think about me; second, when you cross over the Rainbow Bridge someday, I will be there to greet you. Because of what I am, time is not part of my existence. The same holds for you, Mr. Toad. "You mean I get to cross this Rainbow Bridge too someday?" Gabe said, "Everyone on Earth must pass from this life someday. Remember, what matters is that while you live this earthly life, you care for one another the way you would want others to care for you. By doing this, you live according to the Creator's plan and unconditional love. I must leave now. Know that I love you both." Gabe stood there smiling at them, until his physical image morphed into a brilliant white light and then disappeared.

Chapter 55
A Wonderful World

Abbie and Mr. Toad stood there together in the apartment that, even though fully furnished, seemed to be starkly empty without Gabe. They went up to the big, floor-length window that overlooked the river. It appeared peaceful, with no indication of the destruction that had occurred on and near it. Abbie's mom came home from work and went looking for her as she always did. Mr. Toad wondered if their adventure really happened or if he had dreamed all of it. He asked Abbie and she said since they both had the same memories, it must have really happened.

That night they both felt exhausted, said goodnight to one another and went to bed. Mr. Toad buried himself in the soft moss at the bottom corner of his aquarium, falling asleep almost instantly. Abbie was in her mom's bed with her favorite stuffed animal she used as a chin rest. Despite being very tired, she tossed and turned and couldn't seem to get comfortable. She whimpered, thinking about Gabe, missing his perfect being. The invisible world in the apartment seemed to be more active tonight, leaving her with a feeling of contentment. She finally fell asleep remembering what Gabe had said to her: Just think about him and he would be with her. She didn't understand how any of this happened, but she knew that she did feel his presence and love.

That night, Abbie and Mr. Toad both dreamt about their friends on the river. Soshi and Julian were building a new warren, and Julian was helping Soshi to plan and decorate it. Opal was living with Slade, Violet and the babies, and they had returned to their big underground home under the oak tree opposite the big window that Abbie and Mr. Toad would look out of each day. Myrtle decided that Dustin needed more supervision, so she told him he needed to live with her for awhile to learn more raccoon survival skills. She found a hollowed out tree next to the big oak tree over Slade and Violet's warren. Selena was reunited with some cousins and she moved in with them. Beryl completed her nest and was waiting to lay her eggs. Varun and his wife were raising the babies in their lodge. The entire beaver community was helping them take care of their babies, whose teeth were finally growing. Credence Rock was still there, as a source of healing for anyone who was harmed by Grimes' toxin. Juice was in the hospital, and had spoken with Maggie's dad about Grimes' plan to change the environment genetically.

When Mr. Toad hopped up the stairs the next morning to join Abbie at the window, he said, "Wow! You'll never guess what I dreamed about last night." She looked at him smiling her doggie smile and said, "It's a wonderful world, isn't it?"

Epilogue

It was an idyllic day to be on a private yacht in the Caribbean. The trade winds gently cooled the upper deck from the heat of the day as the group of environmentalists sat discussing the news about Grimes' trial for Environmental Terrorism. "We were considering him to be the executive director of our new global initiative, before he abandoned us in the river. It looks like they have sufficient evidence, plus the confession from his friend, to convict him. We never did get a chance to meet that guy," one of the women said. "Maybe, but I did some checking on my own, and found out Grimes isn't doing that well. He might be spending his time in a prison hospital rather than a prison cell," a man added. "He has some neurological disease, I think ALS, that was recently diagnosed."

A female celebrity of the group was applying tanning lotion over the discolored patches of skin on her legs. "I don't want to get too much sun on myself, these spots are getting too dark, almost charcoal gray, not tan," she said to another woman. "What do you mean? I'm getting those too on my arms and legs. I started noticing them a few weeks ago," another woman said. The others in the group stopped and stared at one another. They all had the same frightening thought: was there something it that river water that was now affecting their bodies? It had been six months since their ordeal in the river with the beavers...

Virginia was born and raised in Providence, Rhode Island, growing up as an only child of first generation American parents. She spent much of her after-school time with her maternal grandparents, who had immigrated to the United States from Italy in the first decade of the twentieth century. Their traditional values and her Catholic education were a great influence in her life. She received a Bachelor of Arts degree from Rhode Island College and her Ph.D. in Psychology from the University of Rhode Island. She is the mother of two sons, and has two granddaughters. She is a licensed Psychologist and lives with her husband Morgan, in Rhode Island.